THE ROAD FROM NOWHERE

By

R. J. PEARCE

A CIP catalogue record for this title is

available from the British Library.

www.paganuspublishing.co.uk

First Published in 2016

ISBN 978-0-9930676-7-9

Paganus Publishing

Ruthin

Denbigh

Paganus Publishing

Cover Designed by Paganus Images

STORY DESCRIPTION

The Road from Nowhere draws one woman and three men to a mysterious village where they begin to mend their unhappy lives. Romance and mystery follow as they walk the Tumbleford road.

AUTHOR

R.J. Pearce was born in 1933 in Essex. After a fairly conventional education, he served his National Service in Malaya through 1951 to 1953. Following demob he met and married Sheila, the mother of his three children, David, Lynn and Stephen. He joined the Met police in 1957 and following that he owned and ran his own business. In the subsequent years he worked as a security consultant with a leading company in the field. He became a company secretary and later worked for the MOD until his retirement at 65. He has always been a keen cyclist and athlete, preferring half and full marathons. His passion however is golf which he has played for over 55 years. After his divorce, he moved to Australia where he and Diana lived for seven years, returning to the UK in 2013. In 2015 he and Diana were married and now live in North Wales.

DEDICATION

For Diana, who is the most forgiving person I know.

Particularly with me.

CONTENTS

STORY DESCRIPTION *6*

AUTHOR *7*

DEDICATION *8*

CONTENTS *9*

INTRODUCTION *12*

TUMBLEFORD *21*

SOMEWHERE IN THE ENGLISH COUNTRYSIDE 22

THE GAMBLER *30*

CHAPTER ONE 31

CHAPTER TWO – A CHANGE OF SCENE....................37

CHAPTER THREE - ARRIVAL.....................................41

CHAPTER FOUR – THE VILLAGE ,...............................55

CHAPTER FIVE – SURPRISES GALORE 59

CHAPTER SIX – FRANKLIN'S EDUCATION 67

CHAPTER SEVEN - ENLIGHTENMENT 72

CHAPTER EIGHT – THE WALK 78

CHAPTER NINE – CONFLICTING MEMORIES 84

CHAPTER TEN 101

CHAPTER ELEVEN – THE LAST DAY 103

THE LOVER..*107*

CHAPTER ONE – TOO LATE NOW 108

CHAPTER TWO 115

CHAPTER THREE 125

CHAPTER FOUR 128

CHAPTER FIVE 132

CHAPTER SIX 136

CHAPTER SEVEN 153

THE SOLDIER...*155*

CHAPTER ONE 156

CHAPTER TWO 167

CHAPTER THREE 174

CHAPTER FOUR 181

CHAPTER FIVE 185

CHAPTER SIX 191

CHAPTER SEVEN 194

CHAPTER EIGHT...196

CHAPTER NINE 202

CHAPTER TEN 211

THE THIEF *220*

CHAPTER ONE 221

CHAPTER TWO 231

CHAPTER THREE 237

CHAPTER FOUR 248

CHAPTER FIVE 252

NOT QUITE THE END *261*

INTRODUCTION

John Dough was driving his articulated lorry very slowly down the hill.

He wasn't feeling well and although he had visited the doctor last week who had told him not to drive anymore, he had ignored him. The doctor said that there was a danger he could pass out at any moment and for that reason alone driving a 32 tonne lorry was not a possibility.

John had commitments though. He had his house and his family and his maxed out credit cards. He had to work as many hours as he was offered and to hell with the rest of it. He knew when he was feeling woozy and so would pull over to a café and have 30 minutes rest and a nip of whisky.

He was feeling woozy now, but was unable to pull over. This particular stretch of the motorway had no hard shoulder and the downhill was some two miles long. The cones blocking the middle and outside lanes inferred 'men at work', although these men were yet to be spotted. John kept to 30 miles an hour so that he could keep his concentration through his dizziness and blurred vision.

There were several cars behind the lorry. They were all a little too close to him and each other, for they did not seem to appreciate his slow and careful driving. There had been some horn blasting, but John chose to ignore it. They could wait for a bit. He was pretty sure that there would be police at the far end of the roadworks, they generally were. The police liked to wait for unsuspecting drivers increasing their speed prior to the big cross sign which indicated the end of the speed restrictions. He wasn't going to heighten their awareness in respect of his own situation. He would drive steadily until he could pull up at the services, ten miles ahead. He should feel fine then.

"Woah," he shouted out loud, as his vehicle veered sharply to the left and just missed the barrier. He swung the wheel equally sharply to the right and felt the trailer flick dangerously from side to side as he managed to gain control. He must have blacked out for a second.

His heart was racing and his breath became laboured as he noticed panic rise within him. Surely he wasn't going to have an accident was he? That would put an end to everything. He would lose his job and probably be prosecuted for driving while ill. Then his nagging wife would divorce him and take the kids, she threatened to do it often enough and what little security he had would be gone.

Sweat was running down his forehead and as he went to wipe it away, he realised that his hand would not leave the steering wheel. His fingers were grasping it in white knuckled death grip. The salt began to sting his eyes and the panic rose to a pitch he had not experienced to date.

"Please God," he muttered in a vain attempt to bring himself back to the moment. But it was too late, his right leg had spasmed and he was pressing down firmly on the throttle. John couldn't work out what was happening as the cones came to him faster and faster and his chest tightened.

A man in the car following said to no one in particular, for he was alone in the car, "About bloody time. Get a move on you stupid man." He increased his speed in response to the lorry.

Further back in the line of traffic, each driver put their foot down and soon everyone was travelling at 60 in direct disobedience to the 50 sign at the start of the roadworks.

"I might have a chance of making it on time now," said a woman four cars back. She had an appointment for which she could not be late.

The lorry was travelling faster now and the traffic following did not increase their speed to match. The lorry was swerving slightly and then began whipping from side to side, knocking cones in its wake. The following vehicles began to brake and leave safety margins as advised in the Highway Code.

John Dough lifted his head from his steering wheel.

"Christ on a bicycle," he said as he tried to manoeuvre the steering wheel gently. He knew that he had to straighten his rig before applying any serious braking. There was a steep drop to his left that he had no intention of investigating at close quarters.

The hill he was on was not assisting him in reducing his speed and he couldn't think what to do next. How the hell was he going to make the bend at the bottom of the hill and the end of the roadworks? He tried touching the brakes lightly, but this succeeded only in an increase of the whipping. He spent the next half mile readjusting the steering wheel to counteract the trailer which was trying to overtake his cab. This it would succeed in doing if he didn't use every ounce of his skill.

The drivers of the cars behind were noticing that the lorry driver did not appear to be in full control but at least he was going forward and the end of the roadworks was less than half a mile away.

"I'm getting past this idiot as soon as the road opens up," said one and he prepared his mind for that job. He wanted to make sure that he was the first car to do it because he knew other drivers would be thinking the same thing. Here was the unspoken motorway competition.

John Dough's mind cleared for a second and he saw that he was never going to make the bend. He was going to end up driving headlong down the gorge to his left. There was nothing else for it. He slammed on the brakes and did the best he could with his steering wheel when the trailer suddenly appeared broadside in his right door mirror and then his left. There was a dreadful crunch as the trailer took out cones and machinery from the roadworks and men in hi- viz jackets appeared from nowhere and ran out of his way.

Traffic following slammed on their own brakes as they registered what was unfolding before them. They saw the trailer fall onto its side bringing the cab with it and slide and slither across the tarmac. The driver immediately following tried to find a gap on either side of the lorry, but he was unsuccessful and drove shatteringly quickly into the sideways facing trailer wheels and span around three times before he came to rest in front of the lorry.

Other cars skid and slid in a similar way and many crunched into the rear or the side of the vehicle they had been following. It was the roadmen, now awake from their slumbers, who heard the sickening noise of metal on metal and metal on tarmac and the grinding noises which went on just a little too long.

Everyone could smell the smoke and the fuel and the burning rubber. They experienced the awful silence which follows an accident and the feeling of unreality which pervades all.

Those who were able began to get out of their cars and look around at the carnage. Mobile phones were taken from pockets and the emergency services called.

"I doubt the lorry driver is in a good way," said a man in a suit.

"There will be a few injuries looking at this lot," noted an attractive woman who was lighting a cigarette. She looked apologetically at the man and said, "I'm trying to give it up, but not today."

"We should be helping the injured, I suppose," said another man who had come to stand next to them.

"I can't stand blood, I've seen too much of it and I'm a rubbish medic."

"There are plenty of people going to help," said the woman.

"Oh look! A little dog is loose!" said the first man.

The woman threw down her cigarette and knelt down in front of the dog.

"Oh, you little precious! Where is your mum?" She picked up the dog, which was dressed in a pink jacket and wore a crystal collar. The dog was shaking and whimpering.

"It came from that red car, I think," one of the men who had been standing with the woman informed her. "I'll go and check."

This he did and the group noticed him wince and stand back.

"That doesn't look good," said another.

It wasn't. The man walked slowly back to his new friends and informed them that the woman in the red car was most definitely dead.

"No question," he answered when pressed for information and drew his finger across his neck.

"Oh no! I'll keep the dog until, well, until someone asks for her. She needs looking after." The woman cuddled the dog closer to her breast.

Now, people were running back and to and a man who informed others that he was a doctor and four people who said that they were nurses or medics dealt with the injured.

The group moved to the side of the road when they heard sirens in the distance. The drop to the side of the motorway fell sharply straight down. They were thankful that they had not driven down there during the accident.

"That would have been a proper mess if we had fallen down there," said the suited man. He looked across the gorge with his hands on his hips and studied the scene.

TUMBLEFORD

SOMEWHERE IN THE ENGLISH COUNTRYSIDE

Tumbleford was neither too far away from, nor was it too near to, any large town or city. It was in effect, the perfect location for an English village.

It had a reasonably sized village green, where in the summer cricket was played in the traditional style. The crack of leather on willow and the shout of 'HOWZAT' could be heard by anyone living or staying nearby.

Surrounding the green stood a number of houses, the village pub, the church and a small general store which doubled as the post office. Oddly enough the village also had what could loosely be classed as a hotel, although it was more a bed and breakfast establishment. This boasted the name of The Road Hotel. The hotel had four rooms for staying guests, a comfortable lounge area and a smaller room adjacent which housed the tables for meals. Each table could accommodate four people, though where those guests were sleeping, could only be surmised.

The Tumbleford Hotel was occupied and run by a rather pleasant couple, both of whom were slightly overweight without being described as corpulent. His was a stature that produced a feeling of dependency in the hotel's clients, though in all other respects he would go totally unnoticed in a crowded street. His wife was of matronly plumpness, full of bosom and motherly appeal. It would not be surprising to see the visitor feeling the urge to nestle down into those oh so comfortable natural pillows of delight and without reservation tell her all of their troubles. Both husband and wife looked like and were the perfect country couple. A local widow of proportions in build to the owner's wife was employed to attend to the visitor's needs. She was younger and could be described as attractive in that she had a ready smile and an appeal that would bring her to the attention of most men, young and old alike.

Walking out from the front door of the hotel meant walking almost directly onto the road which circumnavigated the village green. Because of this, the reception door was placed at the side of the building.

Across from the hotel on the opposite side of the green stood the rather imposing church. It was obviously old with a square old oaken double door entrance which led directly into the nave which had seating for some thirty people. It might at some time in its long and distant past have been an imposing edifice, but as time had gone by and other buildings were erected around the green, it had somehow sunk into an insignificant place of worship. Despite all this, there was an air of knowledge about the building that gave any visitor who ventured inside, a comfortable feeling of anticipation and safety.

The vicar visited as regularly as his time allowed, but as he was also responsible for the churches of Upper and Middle Tumbleford, this was not an unusual situation for country vicars. He was tall and had quite a stringy sort of build and his head tended to bob as he walked or talked. In his early sixties, he knew there were no more opportunities for rising above his present position, so he had long ago sentenced himself to being a big fish in a small pond, where everyone knew him and no-one disliked him. On the Sundays when service was held at Tumbleford, he could expect about twenty or so regulars and with luck, one or two visitors. His sermon times were usually kept to the point just before the congregation started to nod off. After many years, his expertise in recognising the signs of fatigue was legendary. He also liked a pint and it was his custom to nip into the pub next door after service for a quick one before going about his parish duties.

To the right of the church was the local public house, 'The Tumble Inn'. Like the church it had all the appearance of age, as though it could easily fall down in the first strong wind. At the same time, there was a feeling of permanency about the rather wobbly looking exterior. Inside, it had all the trappings of a genuine age old construction. Heavy low beams were supported by wattle type walls and the thick oak wooden doors so black with age that at first the visitor might believe they were painted with pitch. There was only one bar.

The landlord was what one would have expected. Large and ruddy faced, and his nose, though not extraordinarily large, was vein lined and a rather prominent feature of his face. Many a customer new to the area would have difficulty in tearing his or her eyes away from this focal point of his whole being. His suit was of heavy check tweed, with a waistcoat to match. From this hung a large gold chain, stretching from the left side pocket to the right. Attached to one end was a very large gold Hunter watch. He would study it carefully for a few moments, then with a 'Morning', put it back in his pocket. This was his opening hours timepiece as the bar had no other. For all that, he was a jolly person. He rarely left the village and was content to be a member of the fairly small community, which made up the population of some two hundred persons. This included the outermost properties and local farmers.

About a hundred yards to the right of the church, the small general store achieved nothing in the way of mystic character. It was probably the newest of the green's immediate buildings and may have only been constructed within the last century. Neither was it the smallest. It had two bow windows, one either side of the front door which along with the windows mimicked the Georgian style. Though pretty to look at, it made it difficult for the owners to present the goods available inside the store. Inside it would not be easy to find items that were daily fresh. Many of the tins would, if anyone bothered to look, be classed as vintage in a world of nostalgia and modern hygiene regulations. Not that that was important, all of its customers knew what was inside, including the tiny section which housed the Post Office. The whole thing was run by an elderly couple who had been there for years, even though they barely made a living from it. The post office generated a very small income, without which it is doubtful if they could have stayed in business. They were part of the village scene and their presence in the shop each morning was an event that the rest of the villagers expected without question. They were in essence a part of the village as was the vicar, the landlord of the pub, the owners of the hotel and the local policeman.

To any visitor the sight of the rather large ruddy faced man wearing the uniform of a policeman, who could at any given time ride his ancient bicycle around the green, might bring back memories of the single constable on the beat. Most days particularly if it was warm, he would stop at the pub. The manner in which he approached the establishment gave the impression that he thought of the establishment as a very welcome sight. Police Constable Brownlow had apparently been there forever, or so most of the villagers thought.

He had arrived there so long ago, that no one could rightly say when he did arrive. One or two of the very oldest residents thought he was the son and grandson of the previous village constables and that there might possibly be a heritage in the police force that deemed it necessary to post succeeding members of the one family to the same location.

Somehow he was never bothered by his senior officers who could not be blamed for forgetting he existed. If he had ever arrested anyone then no one knew about it. He came and he went with regularity and so any person who wanted the services of a policeman only had to wait for him to do his rounds. It was rumoured that on one occasion he had apprehended a couple of the local youths while they were scrumping apples from the rear of the pub. The story went that he had given them both a smacking and sent them on their way, never to be caught again. He was an enigma.

It could well be that had they been asked, no one would know where he lived. If the policeman was wanted, a very rare occurrence indeed, then the villages knew to wait near the pub at opening time.

A number of houses were scattered around the green, all of a different age and style, some had thatched roofs, some were grey slate tiled and only one had red pantiles. To the casual visitor, it had all the qualities of a typical English country village. There appeared to be no master plan in its layout and over several centuries it just slowly became a village.

Or so it might seem.

For beneath the exterior of acceptable country life and times, there was one sinister difference.

THE GAMBLER

CHAPTER ONE

Who was Franklin West?

He was a professional gambler. He spent his early years growing up in an orphanage and became a complete dependant of the system that educated and clothed and fed him. When the time came, this parental system virtually threw him out. There might have been a bad end to his story, but life had a different idea about what should happen to Franklin West.

He was given his name when he had been taken in by the orphanage. His beginnings were the only guide that seemed appropriate. Enquiries had been made about his possible parentage but the orphanage was not wealthy and so such enquiries that were made had been casual at most,

As a young man he insisted on being called Franklin. He hated to be called Frank or Frankie but that would change. He was found abandoned in the

West End of London in a small mews area called Franklin Mews by a derelict couple who were very elderly and certainly had no means to take on a baby. They had the good sense to take him to the nearest orphanage but refused to give any details about who they were. They mentioned where they had found him and promptly left, having no desire to be involved with the authorities. The baby Franklin had been naked, wrapped only in a not too clean towel. There had been no note or any indication as to when or to whom he was born. So the baby had become Franklin West and was so christened by the visiting priest.

Slightly jaundiced, he had the look of the Middle East about him. This never really left him and as he grew he had that very light tanned appearance which gave the impression of radiant good health in addition to the good looks that later in life would have many a young girl and often more mature women, dream of an intimate association with him.

All this was of little concern to anyone in the early stages of his life, but as he grew and entered his school years it was apparent that there was that little extra something in his character that made people look twice. It was noticed that he was a natural leader and that the other children flocked around him. Even some of the older residents appeared to find his company preferable to their own age group. This did not go unnoticed by the teachers and governors of the establishment who all decided this boy needed to be watched. But despite their concern Franklin never caused any problems, rather he solved them by sorting out squabbles between the other children. He was intelligent, did well at his lessons, yet there was an inborn craftiness which most adults missed completely. As he grew into his fourteenth year he was given more freedom than was normally given to one of his age. This was not a conscious act on the part of the instructors and teachers, it just happened. Franklin was considered responsible and so was not watched as the other children were, at least not as often. Franklin realised this and was astute enough not to overplay his hand, early in his awareness he knew just how far he could work the system for his personal benefit. In short, he was a very bright child who knew he had a good future without quite knowing what it would be.

It was by chance when Franklin was seven that one of the older boys discovered his background and decided that it would be fun to start calling him 'Soho' Franklin. But the joke backfired as Franklin decided that he rather liked the nickname and when newcomers came into his life he would call himself Soho Franklin. If he was asked why he was called Soho he would simply say,

"That's where I am from."

He was never ashamed of being brought up in an orphanage and would often explain his background to complete strangers.

"I was found in Franklin Mews in the West End of London. It was the orphanage that decided to call me Franklin West, but please call me Soho."

He also realised at an early age that people listened when he spoke well so he began to cultivate a good accent. He studied hard and was considered trustworthy by the staff who quite naturally allowed him more freedom that he would otherwise have had. He was conscious of his agility and became, as far as was possible in an orphanage, a good sportsman. The facilities in this respect were not perfect but were adequate for Franklin to be regarded amongst his peers as a youngster to admire. His education was sufficient for him to pander to his natural curiosity about most things. So it was in this way that he became a good all round student who was admired by his contemporaries and trusted by the staff.

It was against this background that Franklin saw himself as a well-spoken, articulate young man who could carry himself well in any strata of the society that he was presented with. In time his dedication to this side of his upbringing was to formulate his route in life.

At sixteen he decided that there was much more to be had from the world outside the orphanage so he went looking for work and given the freedom he had acquired was able to obtain employment as a waiter in one of the various night clubs that abound in the west end of London. This in turn led him to speculate on the vagaries of his night life companions. He saw the pitfalls of getting into debt by overzealous gambling or by allowing himself to become involved in any sexual situations, though there were plenty of opportunities. His looks alone guaranteed that and there were enough lovely girls around to satisfy his gaining propensity for a bed partner.

It was also during this learning curve that he discovered his ability to play cards well enough to win more often than he would lose. This in turn brought him to the notice of several night club owners who sought him out as a prospective croupier. He became by the age of nineteen a respected member of the gambling set. He was fair, never tried to bamboozle his employers and best of all avoided trouble from those losing at the tables. Franklin 'Soho' West had become part of the West End scene.

CHAPTER TWO – A CHANGE OF SCENE

He always worked for employers who, in his opinion, took too large a cut from his expertise with cards and this fact eventually got him thinking that maybe he would do better as a freelance gambler. The more he thought about it, the more it seemed the way to go. He had managed to save a considerable amount and so should, if he went ahead, be able to finance himself for some of the middle of the road players if he firstly avoided those who were up for the bigger games. So eventually Franklin left the employment at the night club and started to play the game professionally. He knew that he would have to be careful in the beginning and was clever enough to back off when the stakes got too high. He began to really understand his limits which increased as he learned to adjust to the circuit that played the private games. His social status grew alongside his expertise until at thirty he was a recognised trustworthy professional, always able to meet his debts. Although it was becoming rare for him to lose, there were times when in certain company he would deliberately not win so that he would be called to play again.

They say that all good things must come to an end and so it was with Franklin. His luck began to desert him and he began to lose more often than he would win. It was not a situation that he liked or had experienced previously but he did recognise the signs. There were too many good players who thought such runs of luck would end with the next game and would play on, losing more and more till they had run out of finances. This would never do for Franklin and in any case the scene was becoming a trifle boring with the same faces, the same hotel rooms and the same women trying to latch onto the winner. It was known that Franklin would not become involved, his private life was his own and mostly this was respected by those who knew him.

He was now Soho West, the gambler.

But all this was beginning to wane his interest until one morning after a particularly exhausting night which had gone on until five in the morning. Three

Americans had almost collapsed at the table and Franklin had managed to lose more than several thousand pounds and he decided that enough was enough. He guessed that his run of bad luck was really the result of him being weary of his life style and he needed a complete and fulsome rest. Not away to a five star hotel on the Riviera or some similar luxurious holiday, the holiday that he had begun to take for granted. He decided that he really wanted a break quite different from anything he had ever experienced.

Several days later he was in a taxi travelling to a venue where the stakes were likely to be high. In the taxi he found a newspaper on the seat, an unusual sight but for some reason he could not fathom, he picked up the paper and started to skim through various pages until suddenly a small item attracted his attention. The paper was one of these local ones that no one ever hears about except for the two or three hundred people who live near the village or small town that it represents. Afterwards he would never understand why he had bothered to look at it at all but something had triggered his interest and he gave it more than a glance. It was in these few pages of local chatter which meant nothing to him that he was to find the one piece that would give him a far wider look at life beyond that of a professional gambler.

It was a very small advert, just a few lines that said,

'Enjoy a break with a difference at the Tumbleford Hotel. Guaranteed food you will drool over. No need to book. Just turn up.'

It gave an address in the Midlands and whatever it was that decided Franklin's next move he would always wonder at but decide he did. He went back to his apartment, packed a few essentials, went down to his car in the underground garage below his apartment, had a quick look at his AA guide and off he went. It was strange to feel that he would not get lost, to possess an inner feeling that all would be well and that this was the right thing to do.

CHAPTER THREE - ARRIVAL

Franklin 'Soho' West drove along the M1 till he got to the north side of Nottingham and then took a turning east. Why he took that particular road was and always would be a mystery to him. In fact the whole journey had been a mystery. Why had he even started the trip and why had he driven along roads that he barely knew? Why had he turned off at that particular junction?

His mind was definitely not functioning normally but somehow he knew he was right in taking that turning. He was a gambler.

"I must be insane," he thought. "I could afford to book into any one of the best hotels in the finest resorts in the world and yet here I am, trundling through the English countryside, going to somewhere I have never heard of, to a hotel of dubious quality."

Nevertheless he kept going, as much now out of pure curiosity. He only had to turn round and go into the nearest large town and get a guaranteed high standard of service. All these thoughts passed through his mind as he turned and twisted round bends and took turnings down roads he had never in his life seen before. Yet he knew where he was going as sure as he knew he was still in England. It was a strange feeling, to know that he just knew he had to keep going. His subconscious thoughts told him there was only one destination, The Tumbleford Hotel.

After some two hours of driving along these lanes and roads, his now wild sense of direction took him off the main roads and into a very narrow lane that looked as if it would peter out at any moment. The trees overhung the road surface from either side simulating a virtual tunnel. The road itself now had weeds and grass growing in the centre and it had narrowed into a single lane.

Franklin began to wonder and had actually begun to talk aloud. "If I meet any other traffic there is nowhere to turn, nowhere to allow vehicles to pass. Who will back up?"

Just as Franklin wondered what he should do, he came to a sharp right hand bend in the road that brought him into an open space. In fact it was an amazing open space, because right before him stood a large area of carefully mown grass. On the edge just in front of where he had come to a stop was a sign which read,

WELCOME TO TUMBLEFORD

Around what had now become apparent to him was a village green, stood a number of houses and small properties which at first glance and at second glance were a pub, a small general store and a larger but not by much, country style house that appeared to be a hotel of sorts. As he drove around the green he saw on closer inspection that it had a small sign which gave it the name

'The Tumbleford Hotel'.

Its style was in keeping with the rest of the area. It was obviously old, built of grey granite stone with four upper windows and three ground floor windows. There was a good spreading of ivy climbing up the walls which almost obliterated the sign that indicated that visitors should go to the left of the building in order to find the Reception. The area immediately in front was part of the road way that completely circumnavigated the green. This road went past the store, which had an additional sign informing the reader that it was also the post office. Next was the pub which had a painted sign outside proudly announcing itself as 'The Tumble Inn'. This raised a smile on Franklin's face, as it showed a young couple rolling about in a haystack.

There was also a church.

Outside the church stood a cadaverous looking man in vicar's clothing who gave a fairly desultory wave when he saw Franklin, before he entered the front doors of the ordinary looking place of worship. The building itself could have been fifty or fifteen hundred years old. Roughly the height of a three storey house, the main tower was square and castellated at the top. The whole was surrounded by hedges and trees in plenty, managing to isolate it from the rest of the properties and giving the visitor an impression that it was rarely used except for weddings, funerals and possibly the occasional christening. It was not an inviting church, nor was it distasteful, just ordinary.

The pub looked a more promising avenue of interest, so Franklin continued to round the green and parked outside the open front doors. Going in, he found it was very old fashioned, a good old English pub with no frills and just cider from the barrel propped up on the counter. It had one bar, behind which stood a large man with an enormous red nose. The landlord presumably, thought Franklin, trying not to stare at the nose. So he looked around the bar and saw that there were two men sitting at a table in the corner playing dominos and in spite of the new regulations, he noticed there was a pall of smoke from their pipes hanging in the air level with top of Franklin's head.

Franklin approached the bar.

"May I have a scotch and soda please? No ice."

The landlord replied in a very deep and almost suspicious voice,

"Only stock cider. Straight from the barrel and fresh in last week. Unless you want to try some local cider, brewed in the village, strong if you're not used to it."

Franklin thought about this for a moment, and then opted for the cider.

"Just half a pint please."

"Only sell it in pints." This was said as if he had ordered roast donkey.

"OK then, I will have a pint." I don't want to offend the clod, thought Franklin.

The pint was duly pulled and placed on the counter where the foam over- spilled, leaving a puddle around the mug.

"You will be staying at the 'otel then will you? Because if you are, I will arrange to have it billed to them."

How the hell did he guess that? I haven't even booked in there yet and they may not have room, Franklin surmised. This is a weird sort of place, almost impossible to find and so ancient that I could be in the Middle Ages. What do I mean, it wasn't impossible to find. I just drove here. I didn't get lost, even if I had no idea where I was heading. I will drink the cider and go over and see if there are any vacancies. At that he picked up the mug and tried a mouthful.

"Oh! My God, this is incredible. I haven't drunk anything like this in all my life, it's better than good champagne!" These thoughts whizzed round his brain as he drank the remainder.

"I will go over and enquire about a room then," he said to the landlord.

"I will put it on your tab then sir."

Leaving the pub, Franklin walked over to the hotel and found the entrance at the side of the building. Going in, it looked like many small hotels with a small counter and a bell for attention. A rack with assorted brochures and a visitor's comment book. As no one appeared after a few minutes, Franklin rang the bell and almost immediately a woman appeared. She was about five feet eight with fullness of figure and a rather low neckline on a simple floral dress. This gave him an almost compulsive need to look at the very enticing cleavage but struggling to overcome the urge to bury his face in between the glorious mounds. He looked up into the most wonderful blue eyes he had ever seen. These eyes were on a face that was perhaps a little too full, but which had the look of true beauty about it. Franklin was almost dumbstruck.

"You would be the gentleman from London then, would you?"

Franklin heard her voice with its very slight Welsh accent but was low and incredibly sensuous. It covered him like a cloud of warm air and sent his mind whirling in all directions at once. It was unbelievable. No female had ever had this effect on him before and he had bedded some of the most beautiful girls around. He felt as if he had been standing there for hours just looking at her, from her slightly plump figure to her hair that encircled her face. Her hair was golden, truly golden, and shone like a thousand diamonds in the light from the candles that lit the entrance.

"Sir, would you be the gentleman from London?" she repeated.

"Yes, I suppose I am," he said, not realising till much later that she had known about him before he had spoken a single word, yet later he would understand.

"Your room is ready. I have put you in the end suite, it is so much quieter there."

"Thank you."

Somehow that was all he could think of saying, just 'thank you.' He had never been here before and yet was beginning to feel as if he had lived here all his life. He felt that he had met the embodiment of his dreams many times in his short life, but she had always been on the other side of the room or had always stood with someone else and was just beyond his reach.

"The porter has already taken your case to your room Mr West. I will show you the way. I am called June, as in the month. Should you wish for anything, please ring the bell in your room and we will do our very best not to let you down. I do hope you will enjoy your stay here."

She walked from behind the counter and went towards the stairway, crossing in front of him. Franklin could not help but notice that her skirt which came just above her knees, was close fitting and as she took each step, it enhanced the shape of her thighs and beautifully rounded bottom to perfection. It was of a thin cream coloured material that did not quite cling to the shape of her legs and so had Franklin's imagination working overtime. They walked together along the short corridor and came to the last door on the right. June opened the door, and then stood slightly to one side with her back to the frame as she indicated that he should enter. This left little room for him to walk through and when he did so, he passed so close to June that he could smell her perfume. It was so exotic and enticing that he hesitated for the briefest of moments as he passed and looked into her eyes. He realised much later that everything that happened during his stay at Tumbleford was wrapped up in and started at that point.

"We hope it is to your liking Mr West."

"I am sure it will be fine." Franklin had not even looked inside the room, he was still staring at this wonderful apparition who stood before him. He was so transfixed that it bordered on bad manners. She smiled at him.

'Oh God, this is ridiculous, I cannot keep staring at her like this, what will she think?'

It took a great deal of effort from Franklin to tear his eyes away from her long enough to glance at the interior of the room. It was a good size, well furnished with a large double bed, a large five drawer chest, bed side cabinets, dressing table, two wardrobes, an arm chair and two upright dining chairs by a small, round table. In general the furniture was a fairly mismatched group but all somehow seemed to be just right. The bed in particular was so comfortable looking he wanted to lie down immediately and rest. He noticed the big carved headboard and looked forward to examining it closely to identify the very intimate and exotic carvings.

But just at that moment Franklin's attention was drawn back to June's voice as she said,

"Dinner is served normally from 6 pm but we can arrange a meal for you at any time of day or night. Just ring the bell."

She smiled that delicious smile again,

"Breakfast is any time you come down to the dining room, or if you would prefer, we can arrange to serve it in your room."

"Oh! Yes. Thank you. Err; do I get the room key from the reception?"

"We never lock our doors in this hotel Mr West. We have never had any problems from the day the hotel first opened."

"That's nice to know, just how old is the hotel?"

"It was first opened in the early part of the sixteenth century and has a good deal of history, if you have time later on I would be glad to show you around and tell you all there is to be told."

"That would be really nice, thank you." Anything to be close to you, he thought.

With that June slid past him and walked away and down the stairs. Franklin stood there for several minutes wondering just what he had been subjected to. He had never been so instantly attracted to any female and could not understand why this incredible woman held such a fascination. He wanted to chase after her and almost beg her to stay and talk to him. He wanted to hold her in his arms and feel the pressure of her body against his. He wanted her more than anyone he had ever wanted in his whole life. He walked over to the armchair and sat down, feeling drained of all feelings except those pertaining to the woman who he had met just ten minutes before.

How could this happen?

He would have a shower and perhaps he would see her in a different light. Without another thought he stripped off and walked into the shower just off the main bedroom. Having washed away all the day's travel grime, he walked back into the bedroom to discover that his bags had been emptied and all his clothing was either carefully hung up in the wardrobe or laid out neatly in the chest of drawers.

'Funny', he said to himself. 'I never heard anyone come into the room, must have been very quiet and certainly very quick. I wasn't in the shower for more than a few minutes.'

That was not the last time things were difficult to explain, as he would find out over the next few days.

CHAPTER FOUR – THE VILLAGE

It was still early in the evening and Franklin was not accustomed to having dinner until 8 or 9 p.m. So having nothing in particular to do, he decided to have a further look at the village and maybe sample some more of that superb cider at the Tumble Inn. He smiled again at the recollection of first seeing the quite obvious sign. 'So the village has a good sense of humour,' he muttered to himself.

He dressed casually in light grey trousers and white high necked cotton top which were just enough to keep out the late afternoon chill after what had been a warm day. Walking out of the hotel he started towards the pub and as he approached the front entrance, a large portly man came out dressed as a policeman, although not the sort of policeman Franklin had been used to. No, this one was at least six feet plus and almost the same around the middle. He had a large moustache and a face as ruddy as the sunset. He stood there for a moment looking at Franklin.

"You must be the gent from London then, come to see how we country folk live."

It was a statement rather than a question but it still surprised Franklin to realise that by now nearly everyone in the village may well know who he was and where he was from.

"Yes, it's a nice place and everyone appears very friendly," he said cheerfully and bloody nosy he said to himself.

"Will you be staying long?"

"I don't really know yet. I will have to see how I feel after a couple of days rest."

"My name is Barnaby Wilson and I've been the local officer round here for the past twenty years, as was my father before me. If you want to know anything that I may be able to assist with, then just ask the landlord and he will let me know and I'll come running. Well on me bike, bought that with my first pay packet, they don't make 'em like that nowadays. Anyway that's me, Mr West, stay out of trouble and you will be treated very well in Tumbleford. Cheerio!"

With that he climbed on his cycle and rode slowly away across to the other side of the green and down a side road which Franklin had not noticed before. Franklin could not help wondering how everyone knew who he was, it was uncanny. He wandered into the front door of the pub and was greeted by the landlord standing behind the bar with a pint of the barrel cider in his hands.

"Evenin' sir, pint of the best is it? Fresh in today."

"Well! Yes, why not? It certainly is a really good brew, where does it come from?"

"A brewery in one of the nearby villages, dare say you will see it when you are out walking."

"Very friendly policeman I just met outside."

"He is that, been here forever, as was his dad before him and his grandad before that He knows what it's all about around here. That's why we don't have any trouble hereabouts, comes in for his regular pint almost every day."

Franklin looked down and into the tankard of cider and realised he had drunk over half of it, 'Odd that,' he thought, 'can't say I remember drinking that much, still it's pretty good stuff,' and with that he tipped the tankard up to his lips and downed the rest of it. Then he put the tankard on the bar top and decided to have a walk around the green. He had noticed a store nearby and thought he might see what was available.

No one said a word as he walked out, the two old men sitting in the corner playing dominos never even glanced in his direction. The landlord was busy wiping down the bar top as if he had been serving a dozen customers and not had time to do it before. It seemed to Franklin that he had wandered into a time warp somehow and travelled back in time. He looked around and saw his car outside the hotel 'Well that's a positive anyway.'

But as yet he had no idea just what Tumbleford had in store for him.

CHAPTER FIVE – SURPRISES GALORE

He crossed the green, when it occurred to him that maybe it was the local cricket ground and therefore a hallowed place not to be trodden on by strangers. Yet somehow he did not feel a stranger here, it was as if he had known this place forever. He was beginning to feel at home for the first time in his life.

Walking slowly, Franklin found himself going towards the side lane where he had seen the village bobby go and as he did so he became aware of the church. More so because standing in the front entrance was a strangely dressed person who on closer inspection was possibly the vicar he had seen earlier. His dress was so old fashioned that he might have been from the eighteenth century with frock coat and gaiters, topped off by a large brimmed dome-like hat. His clothing had the dusty looking appearance that only age can acquire and was rather threadbare at the collar and cuffs. This was all worn by a six foot tall, skinny man in his sixties or even older, it was difficult to tell. His face was gaunt and lined and had a pallor that can only be described as dead looking.

As Franklin approached, the apparition spoke in a high pitched voice which somehow demanded attention.

"Good evening Mr West, I trust they have made you welcome at the hotel?"

'How the hell does he know who I am? Do they all have some kind of telepathy between them?' Franklin muttered to himself.

But he openly replied, "Yes they do seem to be friendly there, as is everyone I have met so far. Call me Soho and not Mr West please, because that's where I was found as a baby." Now why should I have told him that?

"That's a place in London then I take it?"

"Yes, part of the West End."

"The West End, yes I have heard of that place. A true den of iniquity it is said."

"Have you not been to London then?"

"Never have, nor do I want to."

Franklin was a little nonplussed over this adamant statement from a man he had only just met. But he was determined to maintain a politeness towards everyone till he established who was who in this most odd of places.

"I am sorry sir but I did not catch your name. I assume you are the resident vicar of this parish, would that be correct?"

"I am Jerrimia Simpson and have been vicar of this parish and two others like it for the past thirty one years. If you are staying very long I hope you will be attending my service on Sunday at ten o'clock precisely. My sermon this week will be on the sins of man and the hell bent consequences. You should attend."

With that he turned and strode into the church.

Franklin stood there for a moment wondering just what other odd characters this village had in store for him. So far this vicar and a fat policeman who had somehow managed to remain at the same post for all his service, after his father and apparently his grandfather as well. Just how far back in the family did the post of village bobby go? Franklin was not that conversant with this system of policing but he felt that three or perhaps more generations working in the same area was a bit far-fetched. Perhaps a local newspaper would give him some idea of what more he could expect in the way of surprises. A visit to the Post Office would give him a clue.

As he approached the shop door he noticed the peeling paintwork on the windows and door frame. The colour had faded and as he got closer it was obvious that it had had no attention for many generations. The paint was peeling back and there were several colours showing, yet the door itself was a clean and very dark purple. It shone like a beacon against the rest of its surroundings and the finish was like a coating of glass. In the centre of this door was a large wrought iron knocker with the head of a griffin snarling at anyone who might dare handle it.

The sign at the side of this amazing sight stated, 'We are Open.'

Being a little wary of actually touching the knocker, Franklin pushed open the door and stepped over the threshold into yet another world of incredible commerce. It was in this way that Franklin entered possibly the most bizarre small business he had ever encountered and met with its owners.

Standing behind the old redwood counter were the oddest couple. A man who could not have been more than five feet tall with a head that was too large for the skinny body it supported, was as bald as a football, shiny as the front door and pink as a baby's bottom. His face was wide at the crown but tapered down to a narrow chin. He had a thin nose and thin lips set in a grin, although he did possess a set of good teeth. But it was the eyes that set the man apart, they were large and the colour of blue diamonds. Franklin had never seen such eyes before, they demanded attention, they said look and you will see such wonders, that all that has gone before in your life will seem insignificant. He guessed at the man's age being between fifty and seventy but he could have been younger or even older, there was no certain way to tell.

Franklin was so transported by the man's eyes that it was not till much later did he realise that the man wore a suit the colour of purple.

Several feet away stood a woman of such different qualities that at first it was hard to imagine there could be any relationship between them but a couple they were. They were so mismatched that there could be no doubt that they were husband and wife.

She stood well over six feet tall, possibly closer to seven feet, not fat but certainly full of figure with a bust in keeping with the rest of her. Standing straight, she would normally have been an imposing figure had it not been for her husband's intently arresting presence. Nevertheless she was a striking looking person with a face that if not beautiful, was without a doubt, a face with classic looks that would turn many a head. There was a certain haughtiness about it that dared you to disagree with her on any subject, yet seemed as though she would be capable of loving the right man with an intensity that could border on the insane. She was dressed in a plain light grey dress that hugged her generous frame, a low neckline with surprising large purple buttons down the front which had been stitched on with luminous coloured thread.

"Yes sir, how can we help you?" The deep baritone voice took Franklin by surprise and he looked round to see who else could be there who he had not noticed. There were no other people there.

The voice came again.

"As you are staying at the hotel, perhaps you would like a map of the area so that when you take your walks you will not get lost?"

'Take your walks', what was the man saying?

By now the realisation that the voice belonged to the small man behind the counter was a bit of a surprise, as was the fact that he also knew that Franklin was staying at the hotel. But then it seemed that everyone in the village knew of him, even though he had only been there less than an hour. But, 'take your walks'. Franklin had not even considered doing that at any time, although now he was thinking that it seemed like a good idea.

"Yes please, that would be fine. Perhaps you have a local newspaper as well?"

"The Tumbleford Tribune would be the best for you sir, though they will have the usual complimentary copy at the hotel."

"That copy may already have been taken."

"Oh! I don't think that will be likely sir. You are the only guest at the moment and there aren't any more booked in for at least a week."

Franklin thought that they must all know each other's business as is often the case in a small village.

So proffering the correct money and saying thank you, once more, Franklin left the shop with the newspaper tucked under his arm and decided to wander over to the pub for a drink. He couldn't get the thought of the superb cider from his mind.

CHAPTER SIX – FRANKLIN'S EDUCATION

Although he had decided to satisfy his curiosity about the wonderful taste of the cider, Franklin was still taken aback when he was greeted by the landlord with a pint of the same incredible cider on the counter of the Tumble Inn, before he asked for it.

"Thought you would come back sir, most people do. But you'll want your dinner soon, so I'll only pour the one pint for you. You'll be in for a real treat there, June is a great cook. She's the best there is and she don't cook for everyone, just special guests and I guess you be one o' they, seeing as you be from that there London place."

This being a long statement for the landlord, he turned and walked to the end of the bar and started wiping it down. Why, Franklin could not imagine, it was already as clean and shiny as new.

Downing the cider with absolute contentment, he thanked the landlord and left the pub before he walked slowly over to the hotel. Franklin noticed that the time was 6.30 pm. 'Odd that' he thought, 'I don't seem to have done much but the time has flown past. I think I must have been in the pub for close on two hours.'

Walking into the hotel he was met by June and he stopped in his tracks. She was dressed in a very fetching waitress's uniform. It was momentous in that it was not modern but could have been from one of the 1930's Lyons corner house restaurants. The only difference was that it fitted June as if it had been made by a high class west end couturier and she looked fantastic. If he had been attracted before, now he was drawn like iron filings to a magnet. It was as much as he could do to prevent himself from putting his arms around her and holding her in his embrace. He wanted with all his might to feel her body against his, to feel those cushions of delight pressed against his chest and feel those lips of pure promise caressing his own. He knew without ever touching her that there had never been nor would there ever be, another woman to compare with this vision of desire.

So he just stood there with a silly school boy grin on his face and not knowing what to say.

She spoke, "If you would take a seat sir, I will bring you your starter."

He didn't care what it would be just as long as it was June who served it and stayed near him. But he was pleasantly surprised when she placed in front of him a starter of 'Fetta' cheese on a base of spinach and a very light mustard sauce on the side. It was delicious and as he took a mouthful of the good white wine, he looked over at June. She smiled with satisfaction because he was enjoying the beginnings of what proved to be the very best meal he could remember. The main course was a rump steak, his particular favourite, done to perfection and nicely pink in the centre. It was as tender as any grand chef would have cooked it. It was surrounded by button mushrooms, halved and gently fried in butter alongside two halves of good English tomato and heated so that the skin just fell off. The whole was served with a sauce that he could only later dream about. The sauce tasted of everything that he liked the most and complemented the steak as much as June's uniform complemented her figure. It was perfect. And to top that, he ate apple tart and creamy custard that simply melted in the mouth.

June came over and as she leant over the table in front of him he had a glimpse between those other two desserts that were so much on his thoughts.

"Is there anything else that I can get for you sir. A nice liqueur to round off the meal perhaps or a brandy? We stock a very good Napoleon which I can highly recommend." She gave a smile of so much promise.

"I think June, that that was possibly the finest food I have ever eaten. Just how did you know what was my most ardent desire as far as the perfect meal would be?"

"We aim to make our guests comfortable sir. Would you care to have your coffee in your room? I could bring it up when I get your brandy. It would be more comfortable there, as we do not have a lounge."

"That seems an excellent notion. I have a great novel and the local newspaper to read and good grief!" He had glanced at his watch and saw that it was now eleven fifteen. "I thank you once again."

With that he stood and casually walked across to the stairway and up the stairs to his room where he found that his blue silk pyjamas were neatly folded on his turned down bed. He stood by the window for a few moments looking out over the green, now dark. There were no street lights but some light did come from a pale moon and a few of the properties, which cast a ghost like appearance to the whole scene. Franklin could not quite explain it, but he knew that there was so much more he was yet to experience from his sudden impulse to drive here.

He was to be so enlightened.

CHAPTER SEVEN - ENLIGHTENMENT

Franklin was tired, very tired. He was experiencing the kind of tiredness that had come over him after an all-nighter at the card table.

It wasn't till he had undressed and put on his pyjamas that he remembered that June said that would bring up the brandy and coffee. Too late now he thought, I will get into bed and all will be well enough. This he did and as soon as he pulled the covers over himself, he realised just how tired he was. But what a meal, it had been fantastic.

Franklin fell asleep.

Or did he? The next morning when he awoke it was gone nine o'clock. He lay there thinking about the dream he had, or was it a dream? He remembered that the door opened and June had arrived with the brandy and coffee. She set it down on the bedside table and asked once more if there was anything else that she could get for him and she smiled that bewitching smile.

He could not bring himself to send her away and so he searched his mind for something to say that would prolong her visit.

"Have you worked here for long?" God! That sounded so lame. Surely he could have thought of something better, he was supposed to be a past master at small talk.

But he need not have worried because June sat on the edge of the bed and said,

"I've worked here since I left schooling and I cannot really imagine working anywhere else."

'I left schooling' Franklin wondered about the phrase 'I left schooling.' It was strange.

Her nearness on the bed was so natural that he could detect the essence of her. His movement to reach out and touch her hand was automatic. There was no retraction of the hand, no look of surprise, just that wonderful smile. He reached over and put his hand on her shoulder and gently pulled her towards him. As he did this, he noticed that she was wearing a simple floral patterned dress buttoned down the front. It had a low neckline which outlined that haven of beauty that so entranced him. He wanted so much to lean forward and rest his head in between that wonderful enclosure. But it was June who edged up the bed towards him and laid her head on his chest.

Franklin was getting excited and it was beginning to show, but he had gone so far he found he could not and did not want to stop. Placing a hand on her breast, he felt her heart beating perhaps more quickly than would be normal. Gently he began to undo her buttons and as he did so, June moved as close to him as she could. She slid into the bed beside him. Her buttons were undone in a matter of moments and before Franklin had time to take a few drawn out breaths she was naked in bed with him. He was also naked and they lay together enjoying the feeling that nothing should be rushed.

He stroked her body and then carefully in case he broke her, he found her more private parts. He moved to that space of wonder between her thighs. She was damp and there was a quivering in her body that gave way to a shudder when he found that one spot that brought her to a sudden shaking. He massaged gently before he tried to enter her and discovered that he could be patient until June desired it to be so. Her hands were roaming all over his body and when she found his erection, she gave an excited cry, holding it firmly with both hands as if it was the eighth wonder of the world.

He was holding her and he was in her. This was as much like heaven as he could imagine. This slow rhythmic movement of her body as she kept him erect and the feeling that he could burst at any moment and yet just as he was about to climax, she would clench her love muscles and hold still for a short while before she began that incredible gyration of her body. This happened several times before he realised that he was beyond the point of no return and he began to tremble and shudder in the throes of ejaculation. June gasped and shuddered with him and they synchronised their emotions right down to the second. Franklin had never felt such a fullness of sexual contentment as he felt then. He did not want it to end and he just wanted to lie there inside her warmth. He was astounded that he could maintain such passion for so long, for it seemed that he had been joined with her for hours as he lay there relaxed and totally exhausted.

He began dreaming of starting again as soon as he could.

Franklin woke up.

He was in bed and he suddenly realised that he was alone. He could smell the wonderful essence of June, he could remember everything and all his memories were intact. He knew that it was all true, it really had happened. He knew that June had come to his room and she had climbed into bed with him and they had made love in a way that only fantasy could produce. But he knew it was all true.

He just lay there for a while before he sat up in bed and thought that he would love a nice hot coffee. He suddenly noticed the bedside table and saw the glass of brandy and right next to it was a cup of coffee, a steaming cup of coffee. He reached over and felt the cup, sure enough, it was hot. He decided to pour the brandy into the coffee and brought the cup to his mouth. Once more he just could not remember drinking anything quite like it, it was bitter and yet sweet it was hot, yet did not burn his mouth. It was perfect.

CHAPTER EIGHT – THE WALK

Franklin was feeling fitter and happier than he had ever felt before. He showered and as he wondered what he should wear, he noticed that his sports jacket and grey trousers had been laid out for him on the chair. His silk underwear that he loved so much, were there as was a smart check shirt and his sturdiest pair of shoes, which had been shone to perfection.

After dressing with care, he walked down to the dining room and sat at the table closest to the window which overlooked the green. There appeared to be no one else around unless he counted the dog which slept right in the middle of the cricketing area. It lay quite still apart from its tail which was wagging and thumping on the ground. Franklin imagined he could hear the thump, thump. But he was surely too far away and indoors.

 It was at that moment he heard June say,

"Good morning sir. I trust you had a good night's sleep" She gave him that smile again. "What can I get you for breakfast? I would recommend the bacon and of course the eggs are local. Perhaps some scrambled eggs would be nice, brown bread toast, apricot jam and some more coffee."

"Yes thank you that all sounds perfect and thank you for the early morning drink it was most welcome." He was still wondering if last night had all been a fantastic dream. No, surely not and yet June did not look as though she had given him the most incredible night of his entire life.

He enjoyed a very leisurely breakfast before he strolled out to the area of the green. He wandered around admiring the simplicity of village life and wondering how everyone knew where he had come from and what he liked most to eat and drink.

As he approached the church he noticed a small lane that somehow he had missed seeing before, it ran alongside the church cemetery, was clean and boasted a cobbled footway, though the road surface itself was of hard packed earth.

It was not a conscious thought to enter the road, it just seemed the right path to take. So it was that Franklin started on his journey into a world he would not forget for many years to come.

As he walked past the end wall of the cemetery, he saw that the road opened out and curved slightly to his right so that his vision was some two hundred yards before disappearing. Without any thought as to why he should continue, Franklin walked on and began to take notice of the terrain alongside the road.

He became aware that on his right side there were hundreds of rose bushes which bore the most incredible lemon yellow flowers. The bushes spread back for some fifty yards or so. There were trees of silver birch randomly growing amongst the roses. These trees reflected the brilliant sunshine which highlighted the tiny droplets of moisture on the rose buds giving the whole an effect of millions of diamonds that have been scattered from above.

Sensing movement, he was sure he could see a small group of fallow deer with the white spots on their backs standing out quite clearly in the bright sunshine.

Franklin casually reached into his pocket and took out a pair of sun glasses. He put them on and the thought crossed his mind that he could not remember packing any glasses at all. He left the thought hanging there while he continued to take in the scene before him. He noted that beyond the splendid bed of colour in front of him, there were miles of undulating fields of golden wheat which drifted over the horizon.

He had imagined something like this so often over the years that to come across it was intoxicating. He stopped for a moment to admire all he could see, the colour, the symmetry, the sunshine.

He had never been particularly religious. In fact his thoughts had only wandered in and out of such debates over the years since leaving the orphanage. He could not be certain that he believed in any higher entity other than a deck of cards. Yet standing here he did begin to wonder who or what had formulated such a wondrous sight. Turning he looked back towards the church which to his surprise was no longer there. All he could see was the road and nothing else.

Where were all the roses and beautiful trees, the masses of wheat fields, the incredible sunshine?

Now here were only scrubby hedges threaded with tangled bramble and bent and twisted old oak trees. The fields beyond were no longer wonderful but were patchy with wild corn and weeds. There was no wild life, the countryside appeared dead.

He turned again and saw that directly in front of him the sun shone blindingly and the roses bloomed and the scent wafted over him in a way that reminded him once more of the night of love with June.

Who was she? Had all that happened last night as he so clearly remembered? It had been so real. Dreams were so often forgotten within hours if not minutes after waking, it was seldom that any dream carried on into full wakefulness. But right now as he looked out across that golden lemon mass of colour and he drank in the perfume of nature, he could feel her softness as they had clung together in their passionate embrace. No. It had not been a dream, it had been real.

Franklin carried on into the sunshine. He could not help it for a trusted voice inside his head told him he would turn back when it was time to do so and not a second before.

CHAPTER NINE – CONFLICTING MEMORIES

Franklin strolled on. He was trying desperately to fathom out why there was so much splendour walking away from the village yet as soon as he looked back all he could see was desolation. Was this some kind of weird test that he was going through or had he been taking a drug without his knowledge? It was possible, though he had always steered well away from the drug scene. He had friends who habitually tried to get him hooked into the delusion. No. That was a sure way to lose all he had obtained. He had a talent for playing cards, particularly poker but any card game that could be gambled on would intrigue him. He had never felt the need to cheat and had never done so. Perhaps that wasn't exactly true. There had been that time some three years ago when he had been with a group of American business men playing for too high stakes. He realised after a couple of hours that one of their number, a rather florid man, overweight and loud mouthed and even louder in his dress code was cheating. Franklin had tried to play round it but the man was really getting far too ahead of himself.

Franklin's ability was sufficient to offset the cheat's game so he was breaking even but the others at the table were suffering large losses but had not cottoned on to the problem, when suddenly the cheat said,

"Waaall! Ma luck cayn't keep going on like this, what about uppin' the stakes to give yeraaaall a chance to get your money back?"

A good amount had been drunk and this seemed like a good idea to them all, except Franklin who realised just what the cheat was up to. He watched and saw how the cheat was sliding cards off as he shuffled and was always the one to gather up any loose cards that were off to one side. The hand is quicker than the eye is a truth which applied particularly in this case. Aces and kings disappeared and reappeared when needed.

The cheat considered himself to be an unstoppable cheat.

"OK, alright by me," Franklin had said. "But you are going to the cleaners my loud and obnoxious friend."

Of course he knew he should have excused himself and left the table, after all he was not experiencing a winning streak so it would have been acceptable to do so. No one would have questioned it but there was just that extra irritation of annoyance about the man that really got to Franklin. So for the first time in his life he began to cheat. He was one of the best and bamboozling a less than expert player was not difficult.

Slowly at first, later even suggesting yet another hike in the stakes, he made sure that other players at the table began to win. He kept his own level with the table at large.

At last the loud mouthed cheat began to get frustrated because all his misuse of the cards was not paying off. Now he was beginning to lose heavily. Franklin noticed the sweat on his opponent's forehead and his quietened mouth.

Suddenly standing up, the cheat said,

"Time to hit the sack. Ah'mm bushed. See yeraaaall' some other time maybe."

With this pronouncement, he stomped from the room, leaving smiles on the faces of the other gamblers. No one knew just what had happened or who had sorted it out and from that day to this and Franklin had not cheated at cards again.

Franklin walked on peering at the roses and countryside, he felt at peace doing so. He was beginning to remember memories of his time at the orphanage, the wonderful times of fun and games with the other children. They had been good times and the orphanage teachers had been fair in their punishments of the errant pupils. At that time there had been the beginnings of the trend to ban any physical punishment of school children. Franklin could never accept that way of thinking. There had never been any harm in it as far he could see. As long as it was carried out in a manner that was not excessive, certainly he had not felt any undue problems with the few times he had received the strap across his rump for his misdoings. In fact it had over the years, taught him that there was a proper wrong and right to life and punishment had most definitely made him think twice before committing any further transgressions.

In the main, those punishments had done him a great deal of good, stopping his childhood indiscretions from going too far. They had saved him from committing far worse transgressions than he might otherwise have done and therefore stopped him from spending any time in correctional institutes. It had worked for him but there are always those that just cannot be changed. Trouble is almost born in them and the desire to buck the system and to object to all authority could seemingly not be overcome. The more the system tried to help the more they took advantage. But those beings who like Franklin, had wavered in that zone between right or wrong and good and bad had generally learnt from those punishments and come down on the side of decency.

The road still went on towards infinity so it was with some surprise that he realised he had been walking for several hours and it was now well past his normal lunch time. At least that was how it felt, his watch had stopped at about the time he had entered the road by the church and so with much reluctance he turned to retrace his steps. His feeling of good will went from him like smoke in the wind with the turn. He could now see the brambles and weeds and the stunted trees. There was no sound except for the creak and whine of a winter breeze. He felt chilly and started to hurry but he could not block out the thoughts that kept coming into his mind.

Franklin did not know his natural parents and therefore could not be aware of any difference there might be between him and children from unbroken and blood families. His family had been the orphanage and the teachers therein. His brothers and sisters were all the inmates and the same as himself. They knew no other life. They were orphans who had a big family.

Yet still he walked back in the direction of the church, not understanding why all he could see was the detritus of the natural world, the weeds and those ever encroaching brambles. He began to wonder that if the world was left to its own devices, without the human race and its constant battle against the worst of nature's growth, it was possible the brambles would become the dominant plant.

He also began to wonder why he was here and to puzzle over the way he had been brought here, for he was certain that he had been brought here, he had not made the choice himself. Being shown the wonders of all those flowers, trees and fields of such beauty then finding he was now looking at ugliness as he tried to see where he had entered the road.

Was he dreaming? No. He had gone down that road earlier thinking about June and her visit to him in the night. So he hurried on, his stride quickening in his haste to get back to the confines of the hotel bedroom. All he wanted at that moment in time was to feel the softness of June's body next to his and again smell that perfume of fresh cut roses.

"Oh God! Release me from this torment I am feeling now, let me know what is real," he shouted to the skies.

With his eyes half closed he almost broke into a run when suddenly he heard a voice calling his name.

"Mr West, there you are. I saw you go along the lane and you had been gone so long I had begun to wonder if you had lost your way. You look a little shaken, can I help in any way?"

As Franklin opened his eyes he realised he was back at the entrance to the road by the church and the vicar was standing there. It was his voice that he had heard.

Rather stunned to find he was on the edge of the green, Franklin saw that it was dusk. He was perspiring yet felt cold and very, very tired. He was not able to understand how he could have been out all day. Surely he had only been in that road not more than an hour and yet it was dusk.

Looking down he found there was mud on his shoes and on the lower part of his trousers. Where had that come from?

"Sorry vicar, did you say something?"

"Yes, you appear a little out of sorts. Would you like me to walk with you back to the hotel?"

"Yes, no that's Ok. I just feel a little disorientated and have somehow lost track of the time."

"If you are sure. But remember I am always available, should you wish to speak to me about your day."

"Thanks for the offer. The way things are going I might take you up on that. But for now I will get back to my room and freshen up. Good night to you sir."

Franklin wondered why he had called him sir. I've not called anyone sir since I left the orphanage. In spite these odd thoughts he started out for the hotel, feeling very weak and hungry. He imagined a nice steak and kidney pudding with small boiled potatoes and perhaps a few Brussel sprouts which had been well cooked in a salt and brown sugar water to give them that lovely sweet taste. Perhaps a glass of that cider from the pub would go well with that. What would be nice a desert to follow? Ah yes, a child hood favourite. Strong strawberry jelly with vanilla ice cream and a thick cream, all decorated with a light chocolate sauce. He was almost drooling at the thought of it all. I haven't had a meal like that for many years. Still I wonder what there will really be. The usual roast and two veg evening meal of most hotels was his best guess.

Entering the hotel and going up to his room he found that his blue blazer and grey trousers were laid out on the bed with his white roll neck cotton sweater, dark grey socks and his black suede casuals. He was so weary that he only vaguely wondered who had been so helpful. He stripped off his day clothes and walked into the shower room. He stepped into the shower and turned it on and while he expected an icy shaft of water, instead there came a terrific slash of hot water that almost stung his skin but woke him up with a start. It was perfect.

As he showered he began to wonder how such a small hotel, miles out in the country could have staff who knew just what was needed to make a guest feel comfortable. This was generally the realm of the expensive city hotels.

He stepped from the shower and reached for the large bath towel and received another surprise. The towel was so warm. He dried himself off, dressed and decided to go down and see what dinner was available. Entering the dining room he could detect the smell wafting towards him of, no it couldn't be and yet it was. He could smell the wonderful aroma of stewed beef.

As he sat down June walked through the door from the kitchen.

"Good evening Mr West. I trust you had a good walk today."

Franklin just sat there, looking at this wonder of wonders. She was everything he most desired in a woman and as she stopped in the doorway the bright light from the kitchen framed her like a huge halo. As she started to walk towards him again, he noticed she was wearing a light linen dress of pale blue which allowed the light behind her to pass through her clothes, outlining her figure so well that she might not have been wearing anything. It was but a moment's glimpse and yet it brought so much desire from him that he almost jumped up and took her in his arms. He thought he had never seen or wanted any woman as much as he wanted June at that moment.

She smiled the enticing smile he remembered from last night. What was wrong with him? He knew he should say something but the right words would not come.

Instead he mumbled, "Yes, yes thank you, it was a strange walk."

"Did you walk along the road by the church? Some people never see it, no matter how long they stay here."

Again that smile as she walked over to his table and gave him a menu.

MENU.

Today's Special.

Steak and kidney pudding, with new potatoes

sweet Brussel sprouts.

This was followed by several meal alternatives but all Franklin could see was the today's special.

How did they know or was it all a simple case of coincidence? No it was all too uncanny but so far it had been all good. All except the walk back along that strange road by the church. Now that really had been uncanny, walk away from the church and all was sunshine and loveliness, walk towards the church and it was all doom and gloom. It was all in his mind but if it wasn't, then some entity that he could not fathom was trying to tell him something about his life and where perhaps it was going.

The sunshine and roses scene could mean a good life and a happy one if he chose the right road, but the doom and gloom side could mean he would be overcome and passed in his so far chosen life as a gambler. If this was true, then he must decide to move on to a different way of earning a living and what could he do? Gambling was all he knew, the night clubs, the private parties, the girls. Every night if he wanted to.

Though on reflection, he realised that he had been spending a few more evenings in his own company by choice, listening to music and reading the occasional book. He enjoyed the chance to wind down in the solitude of his own flat. There was always a multitude of girls who would be more than willing to attend to his needs, all he had to do was pick up the phone and make a call. Before coming to Tumbleford that was his option and all he really wanted. He wanted to be left alone to lead a life that held few responsibilities other than keeping a promised attendance at those card sessions where he earned a very good living.

Then last night he had made love to June, or had he? He was still not fully certain on that score, it had been so real. Then all the other things, the early morning tea, the clothes put away for him when he arrived and laid out for him precisely as required. The fabulous food and the local pub landlord and shop keeper, it was all so strange. He was being second guessed in a fantastic manner and somehow he did not want to let it go at that. He wanted more and more, before he returned to his old world of a frivolous life style.

Thinking aloud he almost shouted, "Yes, I will stay for a few more days."

"I'm so glad you are staying Mr West. Your room is free for the next week, so there is no problem."

The wonderful soft voice that Franklin was beginning to fall in love with, spoke from just behind his chair. Turning round he found June standing there, the light from the kitchen framing her and he found it almost impossible to stop himself from reaching out. He wanted to place his arms around her waist and pull her onto his lap. He wanted to bury his head in those pyramids of delight, to feel the softness of her. He needed just to be with her, to make love to her and no one else for the rest of his life.

Instead he said.

"Hello June. The steak and kidney pudding is just what I fancy."

"It has been a very popular dish lately Mr West. I know you will enjoy the flavour of our cook's version, it's quite unique. I understand you rather like the cider from the pub, so I took the liberty of getting some sent across. Was that in order?"

Franklin sat there in amazement that such a helpful act could be obtained from such a small country village hotel. Franklin did not realise that he could be a little judgmental.

"I could not have decided on a better drink to have with such a meal. It's really perfect, thank you so very much."

June turned away from him and headed towards the kitchen and as she did so, the light once more silhouetted her figure and once more Franklin was lost in a head full of dreams.

The meal arrived and he consumed it with such relish that an observer may have thought that Franklin had not eaten a good meal for days. It was superb, the flavours of the meat and kidneys blended with such sublime excellence. He enjoyed the succulent texture of the pudding mix which encased the whole. It was as no other meal he could remember and the potatoes and even the Brussel sprouts were cooked to perfection.

He sat there thinking that whoever the cook was, she or he would outshine at most of the restaurants where he usually ate. He was on the point of asking if he could personally compliment the chef, when he realised June was standing by the table.

'Where did she spring from?' he wondered. 'I am certain I would have seen her make her way across the room but I didn't.'

Still, he was very pleased that she was there and any more thoughts about the unknown cook quietly slid from his mind.

"Would you care for a dessert, Mr West?"

"I don't suppose you have jelly and ice cream do you?"

"I am sure we do. I am pretty sure that we have strawberry flavour which we could serve it with some extra thick cream and perhaps a sauce of some kind. I would recommend chocolate because it is a favourite of mine and makes a dish taste just that bit more luxurious."

After dessert, Franklin finished the meal with an excellent cup of coffee and brandy and the most incredible feeling of repleteness he had ever had. Sitting there for an hour, he silently hoped that June would appear again at the table.

Soon he began to feel lonely and weary after his day of walking. Rising slowly, he went over to the kitchen door and looked in hoping to see June and the cook so that he could pay his respects. He also wanted to thank them for serving a meal fit for a king but to his surprise there was no one there. The whole area was clean and obviously cleared for the night. There were no dirty dishes and no staff tidying or putting away the equipment. The room was spotless and empty.

He wondered just how they had managed to clear everything away in such a brief period. Franklin decided to go to bed and rest and so went up the stairs to his room. Again, his night clothes had all been laid out and the bed turned down. His movements and wishes were being anticipated to such a fine degree that had it not all been so fabulous, Franklin wondered if he might have considered it all a little too creepy.

Climbing into bed he picked up his book, a political thriller by Clive Cussler. He read for a while before deciding that he was too tired. He put the book down, switched off the light and settled under the quilt.

CHAPTER TEN

Had he been asleep?

He did not think so, but he was certainly aware of warmth alongside him that had not been there a moment ago. He felt an arm came across his chest and he sensed the familiar perfume of roses that was so particular to June. Her body was there he knew that now. He slowly turned until he came face to face with her and he almost cried with pleasure. Here she was in the flesh or maybe not. It was so real that trying to understand why and how was of no importance. She was lying here next to him and quite naked. Her body was a manifestation of his imagination maybe, he did not care because all he wanted was to be here in her arms and be as close as any two bodies could be.

They made love in a slow and careful manner. There were no rampaging movements, it was sensuous and the best he could imagine. As his hands started to explore her voluptuous breasts she kissed him on his face. She then slowly moved down his body and kissed his chest and stomach. She kissed his erection gently before taking it in her mouth and started to methodically move up and down. Moving once again, June was soon on top of him and he was inside her. She had taken charge and he was totally unable to manage his own movements. The eroticism he was experiencing was more than he had experienced before with other women, those times paled into insignificance.

Time evolved into one sexual sensation after another, June was in control and Franklin did not want the experience to end. He wanted this to last forever. June's body was part of him and he was in her. Yet she was all round him, his body was his erection, she was moving, he was moving, they were moving together. He could think of nothing but how his over enlarged member was so deep inside her. She was warm and her vagina lips were wrapped around his spear of love so that he was not able to fall out, no matter how they moved together. Franklin was lost.

CHAPTER ELEVEN – THE LAST DAY

Franklin awoke early.

He was relaxed beyond comprehension. His mind was filled with the extraordinary session of love that he had experienced with June. He reached out wanting to hold her in his arms, to just lay there quietly and feel the heat of her body against his own. But there was no one there. She had left like a spirit in the night. He could still sense her essence with him, the exciting body smell tinged with the perfume of fresh roses. It was so erotic that he began to feel he was getting hard again.

The memory of the previous night was so clear in his mind that there was no doubt whatsoever it had been real. June had been there and they had made love all night. But now once again she had left him to wake alone. She was no dream, she was real. He would find out the truth before he left the hotel. He did not want to spoil his stay by interfering with these wonderful nights whether they were real or not. They were so clear and vivid in his memory that he could not think of them of being anything other than genuine.

So Franklin kept his thoughts to himself and looked forward to each night he would spend with June. Each day he went for walks but never experienced having that first walk again. He would see the policeman who would call out a good and rather jolly hello each time they passed, Franklin on his way to other parts of the surrounding countryside and the policeman usually on his way into the pub. The odd couple from the shop who stopped and asked if he was enjoying his stay and hoped he would return.

It was on his fourth day that he met the vicar again.

"Good day Mr West. I trust you are enjoying our village, we have much to offer the wayward traveller and his soul."

"Yes thank you. I am finding the life here to be most enlightening and relaxing in a remarkable fashion."

"Good, good. Perhaps we might see you in church on Sunday after all. Good day to you." He marched back into his church.

On the sixth day, Franklin decided that he should return home the following morning and left a note on the hall stand informing the hotel owners what he planned.

That night there was no visit from June and he slept alone but without any disturbance. When he woke the next morning he was feeling fresh and able to cope with whatever came along in his world.

Breakfast was served by an elderly woman who gave him his food with a smile and no conversation. The quality of the food was of excellent quality and left him feeling full but not bloated.

When he arrived back at his room he found that all his clothes and toilet items had been packed away in his case in an efficient manner.

Going down to the hall way he rang the bell and a man of some sixty years came out and presented him with his bill. He was slightly built with rather droopy watery eyes but had that burnt looking skin of a man who had spent most of his life in the fields.

"I hope you enjoyed your stay with us Mr West. It has been a pleasure seeing you about the place."

"I could not have chosen better. It has been a revelation and I would recommend this hotel to anyone."

"I'm glad of that sir, have a good journey home to London."

Franklin stood there for a moment wondering if he should ask the question that was uppermost in his thoughts. Deciding he would, he said,

"The lovely lady who served dinner each evening and I guess also looked after the room for me, I would like to say a special thank you to her. She did a remarkable job anticipating my requirements."

The man looked at Franklin rather seriously and after a good few seconds said,

"Funny that sir, I would have liked her to stay but she left late yesterday without a word and without collecting her pay. I gave her a job on an impulse, she looked good and spoke well and most of all she looked just like the painting that hangs on the wall in the dining room. That's the painting of the daughter of the original owner of this hotel when it was first built over two hundred and fifty years ago."

THE LOVER

CHAPTER ONE – TOO LATE NOW

Ted had decided to take a holiday in the country and after some considerable thought as to where and what type of accommodation he wanted, he came to the conclusion that a quiet country village with a local pub or inn would do him fine for a couple of weeks. He had stayed at hotels of all standards during his life and now that he was retired he wanted a quiet, no fuss, bed and breakfast accommodation. Perhaps an out of town establishment, where he could relax.

He hadn't done much during the past few years. Since his retirement he had played golf, kept his garden neat and generally made a happy environment for his second wife. They had married quite some time after his divorce from his first wife, the mother of his children. There were no children from his second marriage and her death had come as a huge shock and it had taken him a long time to get to grips with his life.

He was now in his late fifties and alone, so taking a holiday had for some time not been part of his agenda in life. But some badgering from his children had at last got home to him and he began to think that taking a break from his normal routine might be a good idea. That was how he was staying at The Tumbleford Hotel. It was small really, boasting four rooms for clients, though he doubted if they were all full at one time.

He was taken to a room at the front overlooking the village green. It was a fairly large room and the size was something he would later wonder about because the outside of the hotel did not appear to be much more than a converted house. But he was pleased that it had a room with a view across the green from a window that might have been made in the Middle Ages. When he tried the sash window he found it surprisingly easy to move. The room was, he decided, comfortable in a homely sort of way. It housed a large double bed which was much to his liking as he preferred to stretch out full length being well over six feet tall. He decided it would suit him fine.

There was a wardrobe and dresser which looked older than Methuselah and would have fetched a small fortune in Portobello Road. There was a small desk type table and chair plus a heavy armchair that gave the impression that if you ventured into its arms you would be there for ever. Ted momentarily thought that there might possibly be a fortune in artefacts inside of its carnivorous upholstery, if only you were brave enough to venture your arms down the sides.

The floor was centrally covered in a large Indian pattern carpet, a myriad of whirls and colours. The outer edges of the floor were polished floor boards of that vintage darkness which can only be achieved from years of cleaning and polishing with bees wax. Ted felt immediately at home.

The food that first night, after his arrival, had been well cooked and plentiful and served by the owner's wife. She was a buxom woman in her forties or fifties, maybe even younger or older, somehow it was not really possible to determine. She seemed ageless.

The first night Ted slept better than he had for months and awoke feeling so refreshed that when he went down to the dining area he had a big appetite. Breakfast was equally good, served by an equally buxom but younger version of the owner's wife. So with a feeling of well-being, Ted set off to look around the village.

It appeared to be typical of its heritage with a post office facing onto the green which had been marked out for cricket.

"Getting a six on that small green would not be too difficult," Ted said to himself.

Having played a bit of local style cricket himself in his day, Ted thought he was a pretty good bowler. Past it now of course, arthritis in the shoulders gave him more trouble that he wished for and though he could still easily walk a round of golf the idea of doing all that running and bowling was beyond him. The small general store opposite run by an elderly couple and was well stocked. The big supermarkets had ousted most of the smaller independents but a few of the small village shops survived.

Further round the green stood a lovely old church topped off with castellated walls. Right next door to the church was the inevitable off level pub. Off level because it had been there for so many decades and had settled into a rather lopsided building that looked as if it might fall over at any time. However, it would probably outlast the end of the world. There were huge wonky beams in the ceiling that had the appearance of having been there since time began. It had the feeling of comfort and once a customer was installed into one of the big stuffed chairs by the open fire, they did not want to move until closing time.

Wandering around, he noticed several very old thatched roof buildings which helped give the village green that lovely look of yesteryear. It gave the impression that the village inhabitants rarely went beyond their own small area of land and if they did they were likely to disappear in a puff of smoke at the village boundary. A place where everyone knew everyone else and nothing escaped the eyes and ears of all the other residents. Where the church was the focal point of entertainment and the vicar was the dominant figure in village life.

The owner of the largest area of farm land would usually be referred to as the 'Squire' and invariably acted as the magistrate and arbiter in all disputes. It was in effect a typical English village that had not as yet caught up with the rest of the world. It was Ted realised, as perfect a place as he could imagine and it would do him fine.

The first full day there he did the usual things, wandered around and down some of the back alleys and side streets. He asked at the Post Office for a local map, went to the pub for his lunch and was side tracked there. The landlord, a fairly large man, asked a number of quite direct questions about Ted and his life before he had decided to stay in his village. But lunch was good and the chairs, close by the open fire, were invitingly comfortable. The fire was burning a huge log that would potentially last for days. Set in a very cosy looking inglenook fireplace, it made him feel sleepier and more relaxed that he had felt in many a day. The old men in the corner were playing dominoes but were quiet apart from the clicking of the domino tiles.

So Ted slept.

Later when he eventually left the warm and cosy atmosphere of the pub, Ted decided that there was no need to rush about so wandered off down a side road for a walk before going back to his room for a shower and change before dinner. As it turned out this became his repeating day for the first week. The locals were friendly if reticent to make small talk, apart from the landlord of The Tumble Inn but that suited Ted because he didn't want to talk much either. His daily walks became longer though somehow he never seemed to leave the village.

CHAPTER TWO

It was on his afternoon walk during the last but one day of his intended stay that Ted noticed an entrance to a pathway he had not noticed before. This seemed odd because he thought he had covered every last inch of the village and surrounding area. The entrance was down by the side of the church and was overgrown as far as he could see.

"I might as well see the entire place," Ted muttered to himself. So pushing his way past the first few low hung branches and through the weeds and nettles, he walked along it for several hundred yards. Suddenly it all opened out in front of him, there were no more weeds, no more low branches. In fact ahead of him there stretched a road of inestimable beauty.

It was a road of ancient times, of gravel surface and lined with tall poplar trees. Around the base of the trees the grass was trimmed and flowers of all types grew in a fantastic array of colour and confusion. He just could not believe that he had not noticed it before. From his walks he should have seen it but he knew he hadn't and he wondered why that was so. The trees were so tall and the abundance of colour so radiant, it was truly wonderful and overwhelming. Ted began to enter a state of dreaming where everything was there, but not there.

Ted started to walk.

Slowly and confidently he wandered on, all his worries and frustrations left him until there was no yesterday, or last week or last month. His torments of past divorce and death had gone. Ted was mesmerised by the sheer beauty of everything around him. He was in a world of dream that he had never experienced before.

Yet as he slowly walked on, his memories of all those wonderful happenings began to formulate into the here and now. His mind went back to his youth when as a young boy he had run with his mates through Epping Forest, kicking leaves. They played all the games that young boys fantasise about when they, not Errol Flynn, were the hero buccaneer who rescued the lovely lady from a fate worse than death from the black hearted pirates in the Caribbean seas. The fallen sticks found on the ground became the superb Spanish rapiers with which he vanquished his foes with consummate ease.

In his dreams Ted was Errol Flynn. He was invincible, the finest swordsman alive. He could leap about his ship and on land with the ability of the finest gymnast.

Growing up had been good for him and his home was a happy one. Dad had gone mad, according to his work friends, when in 1935 he decided to buy a house on a new estate. It was not a big house but it did have plenty of room for the family to have separate rooms.

Ted's brother, Charlie was some six years older and as brothers go was helpful and did not usually take advantage of his elder state. Both Mum and Dad were fair minded and in general rather tolerant, though Dad was not a person to cross. There were limits to his modern attitude to life and as a consequence, Charlie was forced into a marriage very soon after being released from his National Service in the army.

Charlie and his new wife moved into a place of their own. Ted did not really like Charlie's new family, particularly his new sister in law. He felt that Charlie had been railroaded into a quick marriage. Still it had been a good thing for Ted as there was now more room at the house and his Dad came up with the idea that with a little change here and there, Ted would be able to have his own entrance to what could be classed as a flat. It wasn't big but it was his to come and go to without disturbing his parents. He rather thought that it was Dad's idea to give him and Mum a sort of early retirement from parenthood. So at sixteen Ted had his own place.

As he walked his memory now turned to thoughts of his first love. She had been in his last year at school and just fifteen and much to the amusement of many of the other pupils they often held hands as they walked home from school. She was a tall girl, which is why they had formed such a teenage crush on each other. Their cuddling and kissing in the front parlour of her home had not gone unnoticed by her parents but for some reason they had not interfered and had always knocked should they bring in cups of tea and biscuits.

It was a natural turn of such goings on that led them to starting to become more aware of each other's sexuality. The cuddling gradually changed to petting and some experimenting. He would put his hand on her breasts and move around so that he could feel her more private parts at the tops of her thighs. It became very passionate but the opportunity to go all the way never presented itself and after they left school and started out in the great work force, both he and she met other young people. It was that which caused the eventual break up when she told Ted that she had met someone else who worked with her.

He was very disappointed but somehow he was not surprised or broken hearted. To him it seemed such a natural turn of events that he just got on with his mates and generally having the sort of fun that young teenagers do.

There were a number of different girls over the next couple of years and funnily enough while walking along this beautifully amazing road, each came so clearly back to him. It was as if he was still there. Girls he had not thought about in over forty years. Those that kissed well and those that did other things well. He became in his own mind the Don Juan, the Casanova, the ultimate lover who could meet and woo a girl as easily as eating an ice cream.

There comes a time in life that can take you totally unaware. You can climb a ladder hundreds of times until one day for no reason fate tips the scales against you and you overbalance and fall off the ladder and crash to the ground. If you are lucky you get away with some light bruising and a dented pride and you can get on with the job. But when you next climb the ladder you take extra care, never again that top step and always a rung in hand. You believe you will never take that one final step because you know you will fall off once more. You hold back just that bit of yourself because there is valid fear attached to that final step.

Ted reached that point in life where he fell off his own ladder of life.

He was a few weeks into his eighteenth year and attending a dance at the local hall that usually attracted some of the town girls and a few from the more outlying districts. The band was invariably pretty good and well worth the attendance price. Ted and his mates were there to dance, have some fun and if possible pick up a good looking girl for the night. Sometimes the girls they met at these functions were good and attractive enough to see more than once but invariably after a couple of dates the novelty would wear off and he, or in some cases the girls, would finish the friendship. There had been a couple of them that had gone further and he had been invited back to meet Mum and Dad.

Ted had a theory about all this and that was take a good look at her mother and you could well be looking at what you would be landed with if the friendship became marriage. So far he had not been too enamoured of these older versions of his love interest so had connived to end the relationship in some way. There were some exceptions to this rule, where the mother was the type of woman you fancied waking up to each day in later years. Sometimes, though rarely, there could be more than enough of a good thing. He remembered clearly one girl, Irene her name had been, whom he fancied rather more than most of his other girlfriends. Her widowed mother, in her early thirties and a very attractive woman, had been OK as far as he was concerned. At first anyway, but as the weeks went by he began to detect an ulterior motive behind the fact that Irene and he were often left alone in the house. Then if mum was at home she would keep well out of the way. It seemed that they, as a courting pair, were quietly encouraged to spend as much time alone and in the darkened front room as possible.

Irene's mother would always call out if for any reason she wanted to enter. Then as the winter months began to get colder there was always a blanket for Irene and Ted to snuggle under on the huge single armchair. It was perhaps the most erotic arrangement Ted had experienced and for a while he took full advantage of it.

One evening when he called for Irene her mother answered the door. Sorry she said but Irene had to work late and would be home in about an hour but do come in and wait. It seemed such an innocent thing to do, go in have a cup of tea and wait for Irene. Her mother was dressed in a pale blue house coat come dressing gown which he had seen her in before.

On a number of previous occasions she had asked him to call her Josie, short for Josephine and he had got into the habit of feeling comfortable in her presence. So he walked past her into the living room and as he did so he began looking down into her larger than usual cleavage. Ted was some four or five inches taller than her and he could not help staring longer than was deemed polite.

He could now clearly remember the words she had uttered to him as if it was yesterday.

"This is all mine you know, I don't need a bra to keep them like this." She stepped forward and pressed herself against him.

Ted had been out with and been familiar with a number of girls but this mature woman had him perplexed and a little frightened. He really did not know how to react. Why should this woman, however good looking and sexually attractive, hit on him in any manner that could be easily misinterpreted .Why?

Were they as a mother and daughter pair trying to trap me into a marriage I am neither ready for, nor do I want? Was she after sex with a younger man? Ted did consider himself to be a man, although he was so young.

The problem was that by this time her house coat had become undone and it was very evident that she had been quite truthful. There was no bra holding up what were to his mind, two very nicely shaped mounds that almost had him drooling down his shirt front. Her hand was on his shoulder and he was on fire with sexual passion when the front door bell sounded and looking through the small glass panel was Irene.

Ted often wondered what would have happened, or what the future would have been had he stayed that day. Looking back he knew he did the right thing by leaving even though it was probably most young men's dream come true. But now he would never know. He had opened the door for Irene, made some feeble excuse about forgetting something at home and then fairly ran down the road, never to return.

CHAPTER THREE

Ah! Those early days of his youth, when there were far more restrictions on a young man's libido than there were today. To get a girl pregnant was a really terrible thing and any girl who became pregnant was treated almost as a leper.

As he continued on his walk he wondered if the young people in his youth had been better off than any youth of today. But still his mind returned to dwelling on his young life and how things had turned out. It was such a lovely place to be walking in, the flowers were so abundant and so full of colour, the trees seem to tower over him as if they were trying to protect him from something, anything. Ted didn't know what it could be, he just felt so calm and rested and he wanted this walk to last forever.

Memories were flooding back to him and he had to admit to himself that the most pleasant thoughts of those past years were the times he had spent with girls. Not that he had not experienced some high old adventures with his mates and he suddenly felt a little sad. Marriage and family had consumed so many years that he had lost touch with most of them and that shouldn't have really happened. Yet he had travelled the world both for pleasure and as part of his work. He had met so many interesting people of many different races and cultures but the girls were dominating his thoughts while he walked along this most marvellous road of beauty and perfumes.

Names and faces long forgotten were coming to mind so clearly. Suddenly he thought of Margaret and her sister, talented singers who had high hopes of the good times ahead, fame and fortune. Blonde and only a year apart in age, Margaret was the eldest and knew more about the art of love- making than any girl he had met up to then. Even to this day he could never understand why any girl should want to go down on a man for oral sex but Margaret was insatiable in that respect and would attend to his needs any time it was not possible for outright sex. But understand it or not, it was a wonderful release of his tensions. She would slowly stroke him to the point of climax then take his manhood into her mouth and gently bring him sensations he would only later dream about.

For a time he thought he must be in love with her but after some eight or nine weeks a better prospect for fame came her way and he was alone again. After her, it was never enough for him to get a girl to spread her legs. He had learnt that there was an art to lovemaking, the erogenous zones that helped her and him to make sex so much more pleasurable. But he had understood her need to get on with her life in the entertainment world, a life he had no interest in.

Funnily enough all these memories were not coming along in any sequential order, they were random. They were jumping around the years like a ping pong ball.

CHAPTER FOUR

He met Miranda after he had gone to a party which he had not been that keen on attending. It was just after his divorce had come through and the idea of spending another evening sitting in the pub with his mates drinking till he was almost too bloated to move, was the lesser of two evils. So he had donned a casual shirt and trousers and turned up when the party was in full swing. He stood in the hallway for a while and when no one seemed to notice him he was on the point of leaving. An attractive red head came over to him and introduced herself. She was some years younger than he was, but there was an immediate attraction which drew them together, like bees round a honeypot.

Their first date culminated in sex. Her breasts were round and firm although she was in her thirties. She had never been married or had children and was a fitness fanatic. Ted often found that after some serious training at the gym she would be virtually panting for sex and once she arrived at his flat, she would immediately undress and get onto the bed. Their bodies would weld together, the perspiration from them both somehow making the whole session so much more erotic. Looking back on those few months with Miranda brought a smile to him now as he slowly walked along the road.

It was wonderful, oh so wonderful, to remember after all these years, events that had receded to the back compartments of his mind. But the road was doing that, it was so peaceful he had not felt so content and relaxed in years. And the memories kept leaping back as if they were yesterday.

Audrey came to mind. He had been sixteen and at a loose end for a party date. When wandering through the high street he bumped into Audrey. They had been at school together and Ted had to admit in the past year or so since he had seen her last there had been a change. As changes go, this was one for the better. She had filled out nicely and carried a full figure with a pronounced bust line. She had lost that school girl look and was a really lovely looking fair haired woman. She seemed pleased to see him and it was after deciding to have a coffee together that arrangements were made to pick her up later and go to the party.

The party turned out to be a bit of a drag and after about an hour they agreed to leave and go onto a local bar. By this time Ted was beginning to think he had a chance of getting her into bed but strange as it seemed there was shyness about her which slowed him down. Their first outing together ended with him seeing her to the door of her parents' house where after a fairly perfunctory kiss and they parted having agreed to meet the following weekend. The next weekend arrived and Ted had second thoughts about turning up. But he went and the evening went well and after a nice meal in a pub, they wandered along a towpath. They were not too far away from his home when it became chilly and began to rain. It was not heavy but was enough to dampen their clothing to the point of being uncomfortable.

With tongue in cheek, Ted suggested they go back to his flat where she could dry off before calling a taxi. Much to his surprise Audrey agreed and a few minutes later saw them walking through the door of his flat. She commented on how clean and tidy it was and made herself comfortable by sitting on the edge of the bed. What was it that he had said? The memory came strolling back.

"I can dry your clothes for you but you will have to take them off first."

Audrey had replied, "I can't go home this wet," and then slowly slipped out of her skirt and blouse. Oh! Now he remembered. She wore a white blouse of cotton and her skirt was one of those multi-pleated kilts that were in favour at the time. The clothes just slipped to the floor and after she stepped clear of them, she bent down and picked them up. She handed them to him as if this was an everyday occurrence.

Her underwear was all white and though not frilly, he found the experience so erotic that he had just stood and stared. She was truly beautiful.

Audrey had stayed for the rest of the evening and it had been one of the more intense learning experiences of his sexual life. He decided that any girl who displayed the shyness that Audrey had shown at their first meeting must be hiding behind some very subliminal desires.

CHAPTER FIVE

So his years had progressed through teenage adventures, both sexual with his female acquaintances or larking about with his mates. He played football, tennis, badminton and some cricket and life had been one of variations and highlights.

As he continued along the road he was not remotely aware of how far he had walked. This day dreaming was brilliant, bringing up so many memories of his past life that had been forgotten. He was enjoying the superb clarity of them and he wanted this feeling of euphoria to go on forever. He even began to wonder if he had been hurt or had died and was in some kind of heaven. These thoughts surprised him as he had never been devoutly religious and had always had some doubts as to the prospect of heaven or hell. There had never been enough proof in the afterlife for him to come to a clear solution on the subject. But wherever he was right now, strolling along a road through a village which may not exist, he was in some kind of heaven that was giving him back much of what he had lost. So he carried on slowly walking and reminiscing.

And still the girls demanded his thoughts more than ever now his life had staggered through to the present day. He thought about his apprenticeship after leaving school, his time in the army and being posted abroad to the Far East.

Ah! Those beautiful Eurasian girls, how wonderful they were. They had been brought up to please their man in so many ways, especially in the bed department. Their knowledge of the Kama Sutra was beyond reproach, stroking a man to the point of near unconsciousness. The sweet smelling oils that were rubbed oh so gently on the skin and the sexual teasing that you knew would finish at some point. They could keep it going for so long that when the final climax came with two bodies locked together, it had seemed like hours of suspended desire come rushing almost painfully from his inner soul.

There were so many girls to remember. Carol, so blonde and slim and so supple, whose thighs and stomach were so smooth and who would lie there as he gently moved his fingertips in a circular motion across her belly. Each finger circle got fractionally lower and as it did she would begin to quiver slightly at first, then quicker and more urgent until they were both so full of desire that the joining was beyond the imagination.

Then there was Beryl with the huge breasts who liked to be kissed right on the nipple during their lovemaking. A man could drown in mounds like those. In truth, there had been many evenings when he had done almost that, allowing the softness of her breasts to envelope his face to the point of near suffocation. Yet somehow when finally he entered her, her reaction seemed to go from her and as methodically as he tried to please her, she was always more erotic when her so voluptuous mammary glands were being fondled. Ted had ended the affair as gently as he could but the memories of such times could not be forgotten.

Faces previously shoved into the recesses of his mind were rushing through his head. Prior to these reminiscences, he had forgotten how many lovers there had been. He had in his own way loved them all, yet had never been quiet 'in love'. He had wined them and dined them, had treated them with respect and understanding. His motto in love making had always been. 'There was far greater pleasure in persuasion than in force.' If they could not be persuaded then it was a definite no.

Yet for all those wonderful times of getting drunk with his mates and fantastic Christmases spent with family and friends alike, there was just one girl who would live in his memory so strongly that there had never been a day when he had not thought of her, from the first moment he met her to right now as he walked along this road of dreams.

CHAPTER SIX

It was when he grew into his seventeenth year that things changed for him, though he had no reason to believe then just how much that change would affect his life forever. His earlier escapades with various girls and their parents made him realise he always enjoyed the company of girls as much as having a great time with his mates. They would all go to a dance most weekends and when they could afford it would make the trip to the Hammersmith Palace where some of the big bands of the day were playing. His life was one of working hard and enjoying himself as much as possible.

It was just such a Saturday night that his life changed.

His closest mates were Alan and Mick and this was the era of the Teddy Boys and Rockers. His mates were not fully into that particular theme, it was perhaps a little too far into the fashion trade image but they had a standard which they liked to keep. The liked to dress smartly and go out in the evening feeling good about themselves and after the day's grind at work they soon changed out of their factory floor image. They spent ages washing and scrubbing their hands to get the grease and dirt from behind their nails and remove the stains of paint and old muddy grease out of the pores of the skin. They had great pride in their appearance in those days which sadly has declined to the 'age of the scruff' in the years after two thousand. Young men just did not seem to care anymore.

On those evenings the three of them were all dressed up and raring to go. There were a number of good dance halls around north London in those days but on this Saturday night it was off to Tottenham to the dance hall Mecca and hopefully in the jargon of the day, 'Pull a bird.'

They had arrived fairly early and were standing around the hall eyeing up the girls, trying to establish which ones were with which blokes. It paid to be careful because some of the more aggressive types didn't like anyone chatting up a girl whom they might consider their property. This was not always the case as far as the girls were concerned and as a consequence fights were not unknown. A girl would act friendly towards another feller even when attached and so some care had to be taken in a bloke's decision.

There were several likely small groups of both girls and boys lining the walls at any time and each discussed the other groups and tried to establish eye contact before the lights were dimmed slightly. That usually signalled the time for the boys to make their move towards their chosen lucky girl. It was much later in life that most of them came to the conclusion that whether the girl in question felt lucky was debateable. Still the ritual had to be acted out otherwise the evening would be wasted. In those days boys did not in any circumstance dance with boys nor get on the dance floor unless he had a girl to dance with. The dancing was in the main a waltz, quick step, foxtrot or as many were deviating too, the jive. Not that the jive was new, the yanks during the war, Ted still thought of the Second World War as 'The War', had really brought over and made popular that style of dancing, so the youth had taken it up. It was, he supposed, a kind of rebellion against the older generation of the day.

Ted was not a great exponent of the art of jive dancing, though he could get by if the girl decided that is what she wanted. His idea was to get close to the girl and hold her close and the closer the better. Because of this the older more sedate dances were better suited to him and as a result he was considered quite a good dancer. He often got the girl for the evening with all the promises of further play later. He would offer to see her safely home and hope to get her into some nice deep dark shop doorway or side alley. In the forties or fifties many of the shops had deep doorways which could hide many 'necking' couples. These darkened portals were soon to disappear as time slipped into the sixties but before then it was so different.

Heavy petting was not uncommon and the more liberated couple would have no difficulty in raising skirts and undoing buttons without it appearing obvious to any passer-by. Sometimes it was obvious that things were getting out of hand, perhaps beyond prudence but the police constable on the beat would seldom tell them to move on. They were good days. There were some pregnancies but in general they were few and far between because the girls were too frightened to go all the way.

On this night however, Ted was just one of the sideliner 'loungers' looking on and had to some extent given up on the idea of finding a girl for a night of pleasure. He had noticed a fairly tall girl with quite striking looks but had decided she must be with some guy who would perhaps not take too kindly to Ted's intervention. Yet for some inexplicable reason his thoughts and attention kept going back to her and after some time he realised that she had not danced, though several times she had been asked. She had refused for some reason known only to her.

Ted wondered why such a 'looker' should constantly refuse to dance having obviously paid to get in. Still he stayed where he was until it was nearly the end of the evening and eventually with the thought that she could only say no to him as well, he wandered over and asked if he could have the next dance as it was a waltz.

It was with some surprise to him that she said yes. Close up he realised that she was just as he had thought from across the hall. She was about 5ft 9ins tall with a figure that was well proportioned to her height. Her face had a singularly fresh beauty resembling Gina Lollobrigida, she was all that a boy could wish for. She wore a simple white blouse and one of those fashionable wrap around skirts in a pale shade of blue. He thought she was possibly the most gorgeous looking girl he had ever seen. He led her onto the dance floor and placed his hand on her waist and as he held her hand to start the dance, he had a feeling of such pure joy that it was almost frightening. He almost forgot to move when the music crept into the first few bars and stumbled a little before getting into the rhythm.

As the dance progressed he managed to ask her name and was delighted when she said, "Its Jane." Why he should be so pleased with such a simple answer he just couldn't imagine, but delighted he was. Telling her his name was Ted just did not seem right but Jane smiled and commented that it was an easy one to remember.

They continued to dance together for the next few dances till it came to the last waltz when Ted asked if he could take her home. His insides were in turmoil, he felt that if she had said no he would have been the most disappointed person in that dance hall and so it was with the most exhilarating sense of relief when Jane agreed to him walking home with her. He waited by the front entrance while she collected her coat and said goodnight to her friend. Jane only went from his sight for less than ten minutes, but that had seemed the longest time he had ever experienced. Suppose she had changed her mind. Had he missed her and she had already left, maybe thinking he had left without her. The relief he felt when she came over to him and said, "Shall we go?" was inexpressible, he was having feelings he could not explain.

Ted thought about that moment for a while as he strolled along this wonderfully picturesque road. He now knew from experience, that what he felt that first night was the beginning of a love that would torment him for the rest of his life.

It had started out with just another evening at the dance hall with an idea of meeting another girl, maybe taking her out a few times then a parting, usually by some kind of mutual consent. Yet by the evening's end he had shaped the rest of his life. He hadn't known then just what an impact that evening was to have on him and even now, as old as he was and with all his history of world travel and all the experiences that he had gone through since then, he knew there never would be another love like that.

Meeting followed meeting, as each of them struggled to understand how they both felt this way. Telling each other they were in love was somehow not enough, their love for each other was sealed, the first time that they kissed. It had been such a natural thing to do after taking her home from the dance. To kiss her good night and when their lips met just fractionally it been such a shock to find that this was all he wanted from life.

They had stopped at the corner of the road leading to the house where she lived with her parents. She had already agreed to meet him again and he leant forward to hold her gently and kiss her. As he did so, his arms moved around her shoulder and there was reciprocation on her part. That first kiss was to be no more than that, the first kiss of two comparative strangers but neither of them wanted it to end so quickly They just stood there holding each other for a few minutes, oblivious of the cold that was penetrating through their coats and shoes. It was a magical moment of such magnitude that Ted could not believe it was happening.

The days and weeks went by and with them the constant need to express their love for each other. Their kissing had progressed to fondling her breasts and holding against each other as tightly as possible. This was not the lust of previous girls, something had happened between them that they could not avoid. They became as much in love as two young people could be. He took her to his home to meet his parents and he was introduced to hers. Often when her mother and father had decided to retire for the night, Jane and Ted were left alone in the lounge and these times were precious to them. Though Ted had his flat, somehow the thought of being there alone bothered them and it became a tacit agreement that if they were married then that would be the time to enter into such an arrangement.

Yet there did come a time when the urgency of the moment really got the better of them. They had been out to the cinema and had seen the films through to the very end of the night's showing. Walking slowly, they were on their way back to Jane's home and had stopped a few times to kiss and hold each other, neither wanting the evening to end. It was a cold evening and when they were close to home they both realised that they were beginning to shiver and as strong as their love was it had its limitations. Jane insisted he go in and have a warm drink before leaving.

On entering it was apparent that the rest of the family had gone to bed, so being as quiet as possible they made a warm drink and went into the front room where there was less chance of any noise disturbing the rest of the household, which included her mother and father and two younger sisters aged twelve and six. There had been an older brother of the family but he had gone over to Australia where he had hoped to make a good life for himself. Taking on a job as a long distance driver of one of the lorry trains so indicative of that country, he had just a few weeks earlier met with a fatal accident in a crash on one of the then dirt roads. This loss was still very much in the minds of all the family and of course Jane was constantly reminded of it. It was this feeling of despair that still pervaded over the family which perhaps was the reason for how the rest of the evening went.

They snuggled down on the big three seater settee and because the fire had burned down they pulled a settee blanket over them to keep warm. The kissing and petting started, Ted slid his hand up inside her jumper and with the dexterity he had mastered over the years, undid her bra so that he could more easily fondle her breasts. By this time they were lying side by side along the length of the settee, their bodies pressed so tight together that the only thing separating them was the thickness of their clothing. This made them both fully aware of how they were feeling. After a while Ted allowed his hand to move slowly down to Jane's midriff and then onto her belly onto her navel.

The wrap around skirt had clips on the side which he managed to undo with no effort. With her skirt falling away to the side, he saw such beauty before him and he carefully lowered his head to kiss her breasts and gently suck her nipples. It brought on him the absolute need to go further than before.

Caressing her tummy he began to sense the bush between her thighs and carefully massaging her there, he realised Jane was as excited as himself. Her body moisture was allowing his fingers to do amazing things to her. She reached down and shakily undid his belt and pushed his trousers down to expose his very erect manhood which she then held onto as if not knowing what next to do.

Ted was beside himself with desire, he raised himself up and looking straight into her eyes said,

"Are you sure?"

In response Jane reached up and pulled him tightly to her. Ted arranged her position on the settee and allowed himself to enter her. It was the most sublime sexual moment of his hitherto life. He had just enough sense to withdraw before he climaxed, even though every fibre of his being was telling him to stay right there for the rest of his life.

They soon became engaged and though they both wanted to continue making love as they had that night, the opportunities were not presenting themselves. They tried to devise several schemes whereby they could continue and eventually decided to ask her mother for permission to go away for the weekend with promises to behave. When asked, her mother had agreed with only slight reservations and Jane and Ted realised that Mother knew exactly what was happening. She was resigned to the fact that her daughter was a grown woman and no amount of objections would stop her from acting as any grown woman.

So it was that a few weekends later Jane and Ted boarded the coach for the coastal town of Southend. After their arrival they found a bed and breakfast lodging where the landlady did not seem to mind that they were so young. The room was fairly large and ordinary and though it had a sink in the corner they had a trip along the landing to use the toilet. But to Ted and Jane it represented a place as close to heaven as they could expect. The first night they were exceptional in their lovemaking, exploring each other's bodies, kissing where they had never thought to kiss before. Ted had his face firmly planted between Jane's thighs while Jane held his manhood until he almost cried out loud with frustration before she succumbed to his entry to paradise.

It was a wonderful time to remember and even now as he slowly walked on, with the scent of the flowers he could clearly see and smell the odour of her to this day. The combined perfumes of all the mixed flowers by the roadside seemed to give off the wonderful musky smell of love that two people who were so much in love would generate.

Ted shook his head. He would never forget her, he would love her till time ended.

Where she was now? He had no idea. Not long after that weekend he had been called up for National Service. Drafted into the army he had completed his training and been posted to the Far East where he spent the next two years. He had never been much of a letter writer, not in those days, so his postal efforts were few and far between. He had written a few and received many letters in return.

His time in the army, particularly so far from home, had brought about many changes in his attitude towards life. Thinking about it now he realised that in some ways he had just grown up. He had seen dead bodies, it did not matter that they had been the enemy, they were dead people who at one time had been alive. They had been born of woman, had gone through childhood, played with toys, gone to work and no matter how hard their life had been they had managed to get through until one day out in the jungle they had met a bullet and that was that. They were dead. It was not always one sided, army friends had also been killed or injured.

When Ted was eventually discharged from the army he went home, perhaps with the vain hope that things would get back to normal but normal was not on the agenda that year. His father, usually the picture of health had been ill for some time but his mother had not written to tell him. She said he had not wanted to worry him. He could have shouted at her.

"Mum, I have been out to the Far East and back. During going there and arriving back I have been shot at and I have shot at other people. Why do you think I couldn't cope with worry?"

He didn't say that of course, he had just put his arm round his mother's shoulders and said,

"I understand Mum."

So it happened that several days went by and he had still not called Jane. Looking back he could not believe he had been so stupid. A girl he had sworn to love forever and he had not called her after nearly two years being apart. Ted was so mixed up in his mind back then, what he had seen and done for his country had altered him without him realising. In his later years he knew that as a young twenty year old, he had not coped well with the side effects of living on a knife edge for so long. It was too late now.

The turning point came when three days after his return, he went for a walk to the small local shop at the end of his road and as he approached the junction who should he see getting off the bus but Jane.

Ted stopped walking and stared, somehow he didn't know what to say or do. He had not seen her for almost two years and he felt like a stranger. There was no gut churning emotion that he imagined he ought to feel. Jane was still lovely as ever, yet somehow that thought slipped through his mind like a sieve. She was a stranger. He was a stranger. They stood looking at each other for several minutes till Jane slowly walked towards him and said,

"Hello Ted."

He replied in the same strained voice. He could remember it clearly now, so many years had passed and with the clarity of his current thoughts he became aware that his stroll along this beautiful road had also come to a stop. He found himself crying, not loudly but that type of soft sob which comes from knowing that in one stupid historical moment in his past, he had wrecked his whole future.

Both of them had wandered along together for a while, not really knowing what to say. They made a tacit agreement to meet later in the week and Jane got on a return bus.

That later meeting did take place and Jane had offered to give him the engagement ring back but he refused.

He had never seen her since but he loved her now as an old man as he had as a young man.

Too late.

Far too late.

CHAPTER SEVEN

Ted stood still in this most beautiful of places, where this road of wonder had made his memories so acute.

This Road had given him so much in a matter of a few hours, just one afternoon when all those people he had known had come flowing through his mind like a mountain stream.

Those good mates with whom he had spent some hilarious times.

Most of all, the girls. He had loved them all in some way but he had never loved with so much passion as was his love for Jane…………

Too late now.

He found his way back to the hotel and told the woman at the desk that he was leaving tonight.

"I thought you were here until the morning sir?"

"I was," he told her. "But I think I just want to go home now."

"Not enjoying yourself sir?"

"I was but too many memories have come to my mind and I don't want to think of them anymore. I'm coming to the end."

"That sounds a bit dramatic sir."

"Possibly. But I know that before long I shall be starting a new adventure. From the beginning and perhaps I shall make some different decisions this time round."

"Well we.ve enjoyed having you here. Good luck on your journey. I'll have your bill ready for you when you come down again."

THE SOLDIER

CHAPTER ONE

Johnathon Edward Spencer-Smith was fed up.

He was more than fed up, he was downright distraught. He had had it. Everything that could go wrong on this particular day had gone wrong, not just wrong, that was putting it mildly. It had been chaotic.

Johnathon was nicknamed 'Jess', because of his initials. At school one of the other kids had realised there was fun to be had in thinking up such idiot schemes, so he had been forever stuck with the name. In every situation he had been in over the years there was always some clever sod who would notice the initials and then it would catch like wildfire. He had never liked it, he thought it was a bit effeminate but wherever he went in life someone, some wag in the group had managed to see the name 'Jess' in his full name. He had loved his mother but there was a small part of him that blamed her for the initials.

His father had been a Smith but when he married his mother, she had insisted on having her maiden name included, hence Spencer-Smith. It had been pure snobbery on her part. She was trying to upstage the neighbours, before they had even moved in to their matrimonial home. Jess supposed it had been that which influenced his life, having that little bit of one upmanship on anyone who came into his life.

His earlier memories were not very clear, the earliest being possibly around the age of three. He could remember having long curly hair and he rather thought now that his father would have had it cut much sooner, rather than waiting until Jess had arrived at his first primary school. Jess arrived home that first school day very upset after being teased over his blonde curls. Whether his mother had cried seeing her youngest virtually scalped was not a clear image he could summon. It was possible that she had been affected by the sight of all those strands of hair, which had so adorned her youngest suddenly lying on a heap on the floor. Much later in life he had returned home shorn down to a skinhead.

On his first day at primary school there occurred an incident worth telling, at least from his father's point of view. Jess had been taken to school and left in a class with the teacher. Not knowing any different when lunch break came he had assumed that was it for the day and had promptly walked home. His mother almost had hysterics seeing him coming up the garden path. He had of course been taken back for the afternoon session.

However, right at this time Jess was fed up. He was now fifty one years old, reasonably fit although going grey at the temples, which gave him a rather distinguished appearance. Standing just six feet tall in his stockinged feet he could be described as well-built but not heavy looking. Over the years he had grown beards and several moustaches but had always reverted to being clean shaven. His opinion about why men grew such hairy pieces on their faces was that it would hide a seemingly weak chin or spotty complexion. He chose to ignore the fact that it was quite natural for some men to sprout fuzz all over their most prominent feature.

Jess had retired from the army some fifteen months prior but was now a bachelor again after a messy divorce. He still couldn't believe how the system worked. He really had been the innocent party in the whole affair. All the evidence he had gathered was not worth a tinker's cuss when it came to the division of the spoils. Twenty four years of marriage he had put up with. Now it was all at an end.

Jess was fed up. After leaving the army he had taken some part time work in an office storage company but he could not get any enthusiasm for the tasks put before him for the coming day. The mundane clerking work, saying, 'Yes sir,' to men he would have had as lackeys in the army. The same people who would have been lucky to be employed in similar positions in his old unit. He could see them now. They would arrive at the office at nine sharp, hang up their coats on the stand in the corner and sit down behind their, oh so important desk. The bigger the desk the more important they considered themselves.

God, how he had started to despise them with their self-opinionated looks when they spoke of houses they owned, the new garden furniture bought at

Harrods or some other up market establishment. Then there was 'The Wife' or 'The Little Woman' or 'The Other Half'.

Rarely would they refer to their wives by their Christian names, as if they were partly ashamed of who they had married and by association no one would question whether they thought that they considered they had married beneath them. Pompous pricks.

It was a little after he had been there for about six months when arriving at work one morning he had been summoned into the inner precinct of the departmental manager's office and had been given a dressing down over some extremely minor incident from the day before.

"It came to my notice yesterday you were sitting at your desk in rolled up shirt sleeves. At this office we have a certain standard of dress that has to be adhered to at all times. It sets a bad impression to the younger staff to see middle aged workers ignoring such protocol."

'Middle Aged Workers,' 'Standard of Dress.' What was the stupid man on about? The silly old fool had no conception of dress standards. It had been hot enough to fry eggs on the car bonnet. The air conditioning only worked properly in the 'Inner Sanctum.' Jess had stood there for a few minutes then quietly and with the forceful manner he had not used since leaving the army said,

"When you have finished speaking through your arse, perhaps you will take a look at my resume you will then understand why I am leaving this place right now and why beyond that, I will not lower myself with talking further to you."

Turning, Jess had walked back to his desk, picked up his personal bits and simply walked out. The moment he stepped out from the front entrance he knew he had done the right thing. He felt completely relieved of all tension. He walked along the street quite pleased that he had not reacted in any other way, other than in the manner of quiet reason.

That was then, this was now and he was fed up. Strolling to the newsagent he bought a newspaper and read through the sports pages to start with. Not that there was any one particular sport he was following but it was just one of those things he always did when picking up a newspaper. He started from the back page and slowly wandered through to the front page. Nor had he read the headlines when he bought the paper, he didn't want to read the more depressing news before he had the chance to feel good about something.

This morning he was down at heart and morale, even his morning breakfast of muesli had tasted more like dry straw with weird bits in it. He had stared at the half eaten dish of promised goodness and saw seeds in there that with all his world travels he had never seen before. There had been stringy bits that would have taken a chemist to define their origins, probably only then with a large research laboratory behind him. The he had read the label on the orange juice bottle. The stuff inside that he had been drinking for his health was described under ingredients with so many letters of the alphabet and chemical names that he felt like tipping the lot down the sink as a cleaner of drains. Wonder what it did to his stomach?

So here he was, sitting in a park reading the paper from back to front. As he casually turned each page of sports news then into the advert pages, dozens of pages advertising for people with qualifications that could only be obtained from time yet they did not want anyone who was old enough to get the necessary experience that they deemed was essential for holding down the post described.

Onto the pages of more adverts for houses, flats, apartments, cottages in the country from Tottenham to Timbuktu, holidays covering a simple bed and breakfast seaside town house to the more luxurious method of transport. He thought for a moment that sailing the seas and oceans of the world on a cruise liner might be the answer to his boredom. This interested him for a time, reading all the reasons why everyone should take a cruise with this shipping line rather than with the competitor on the previous page. They all sounded incredibly exotic but he had been to many of the places so eloquently described and he could tell anyone who would listen that often the quaint villages were smelly slums with odours that would create a visit from the health inspector if they came from your own house.

He ventured into the middle pages of the newspaper and onto the stories of new writers, old artists, working in oils, pastels, charcoal or whatever medium the individual thought would create a demand for his or her particular style of artistic talents. The stories and articles of interest to someone out there somewhere, though he couldn't imagine where or whom. Eventually he reached the front pages with the international news, warnings of global financial collapse, dramatic climatic horrors or earthquakes and flooding. Forest fires, shootings and murders most foul. It was all very depressing, as if he wasn't feeling fed up enough he could do without the world coming to an end right at his front door.

He threw the paper down onto the bench beside him in some frustration. There was a slight breeze blowing and after a few minutes it ruffled the pages, almost tossing them off the bench. Jess reached over and grabbed then before they flew all over the park. Just as he was about to screw the sheets of news and disasters up before tossing them into the waste basket, his attention was drawn to a small advert in the holiday page. Not very large, just five lines.

'Stay at The Tumbleford Hotel for a comfortable homely atmosphere. Good food, comfortable beds. Relax in the middle of the English countryside. Become yourself again. No need to pre book. Just arrive. Always rooms available in The Tumbleford Hotel, Lower Tumbleford.'

Funny he hadn't noticed that advert before, he was sure he would have noticed it. Still it's not a bad idea to get away for a few days or a week even. To relax completely, be made a fuss of, go for walks, and get some easy exercise. Yeah! That seems to be the ticket, just what his inner feelings had been telling him to do. A decisive thought at last. He had not realised until this minute that the days since his retirement had been so incomplete, so lacking in action and regimentation that he had become – bored.

Going home he packed clothes and toiletries, deciding to take his wet razor and shaving brush and soap for a possible two weeks stay. These days he normally used an electric razor, but he was going to the country and you never knew with these out of the way places. Looking up Tumbleford on the map, Jess closed up his home and without telling anyone where he was headed, began his journey to this promised land of tranquillity. Or at least that was how he began to think of it. Yes, it was the right thing to do. Get away, get his thoughts and life in perspective then come back and start to lead a positive life again. He felt more exhilarated than he had for months.

CHAPTER TWO

He continued this line of thinking during the drive of just short of four hours he came to Tumbleford.

His approach to the village of Lower Tumbleford after leaving the motorway was through a series of narrow lanes that seemed to get narrower every time he came to a junction. The map he was following was an old ESSO map, so old that it was almost a collector's item. Still it did seem to be accurate. So it was, that after about nine turns, Jess found himself driving into the centre village, in fact he almost drove onto the green. He just couldn't believe he was where he had planned to be.

Here was the green and surrounding it was a motley collection of houses, cottages and other miscellaneous buildings making an almost full circle of properties. It resembled the style of the middle ages and they were expecting to be the target of raiding parties from other nearby hamlets coming to steal away their young females. The only semblance of life was a rather large marmalade tom cat which was slowly ambling across the middle of the green.

He sat in his car for ten minutes or more and just stared, half expecting to see one of the upstairs windows burst open and some selfish sluttish type woman throw out the night waste and effluents into the roadway below. Jess had a fairly fertile imagination and was drumming up in his mind all kinds of scenarios of years long gone when he noticed a large policeman stepping out from one of the larger architectural creations. This apparition of days gone-by called back over his shoulder.

"See yer termorrer."

Jess began to believe he had missed a turning and somehow been transported back in time. Then he saw the sign right outside the place where the policeman had exited. The sign was poorly painted and depicted a figure of a man with a half-naked female of quite generous proportions falling into a largely loosely erected haystack. The sign read, 'The Tumble Inn'. Jess had to smile at the imagination of the artist, whoever he may have been.

Slowly the rest of the properties started to come into focus, the very old church with its wonderfully old front doors and the pub or inn, depending on a person's perspective of the scene before them. In this instance Jess decided that pub was a more appropriate term. Gazing round he noticed a double bow fronted building that appeared to be the local store, which obviously housed the post office, the assumption made clear when he noticed a 'Post Office' sign hanging above the single multiple glass panelled door sighted right between the two bow windows. He was to realise later that this was by far the newest of the buildings that circumnavigated the village green but just at that moment in his surprise and obvious pleasure it was not that apparent to him.

Allowing his eyes to work their way around the properties he could only make out two other junctions into the village. They were to his right and the one nearest was just a few houses away and Jess could barely make out the name,

'The Alleyway'

The first building the other side of The Alleyway, was a two storey place with six sash style windows to the front, three up and three down. In between these two rows of windows, a sign proudly stated that this was,

'The Tumbleford Hotel'.

It was not a large place, though somewhat bigger than the others round the green. The church was marginally taller he thought, though that was a debatable point. Maybe the pub also had some pretensions as to being the leader of any such contest. It was all academic at this stage, just one of those thoughts that crossed his mind, born no doubt from his years of military training. Driving over to the hotel he found that the main entrance was at the side. It was not very imposing and just a single red painted door with the words, 'Reception, please enter,' written in white script on the centre panel.

He pushed open the door and found himself in a small entrance lobby which housed a collection of pamphlets in a rack on the wall. Straight ahead was another door and to his right there was a hatch which opened into another cubby hole room. This apparently doubled as the reception and the hotel's office. At this moment it was empty but just as Jess was about to hit the bell provided for attention the door marked private opened and a woman stepped into the hallway. She was not tall, about 5 feet 6 inches in height with a figure that could only be described as matronly. Full bosomed and narrow waisted, she would probably be anything from thirty to fifty years old. Jess couldn't decide at first glance, yet it was strange that he had a sudden urge to put his arms around her and hug her as if she was the long lost sister he never had. She smiled and he thought it was one of the most comforting smiles he had ever seen.

"You must be the gentleman from the city, do come in, your room is ready. I will show you up. It is in the back as I am sure you would prefer it nice and quiet. You will have a wonderful view, especially first thing in the morning with the sunrise over the valley."

It wasn't till much later that Jess realised that she had known he was coming, or had she? The advert had said no need to book and he was pretty certain that he had not phoned prior to his departure. Her voice had a certain melodious tenor to it that the thought did not stay with him then. It all seemed so right, the old world village with its collection of houses and buildings of such ancient times, even the bobby coming out of the pub and riding away on his bicycle. It was all so very yesteryear.

Jess suddenly became aware that the woman had turned and was holding open the door as she ushered him through. He watched her as she swished past him to the bottom of the staircase.

"Follow me," and up the stairs she went to the second door on the left. Jess noticed it did not have a number. Instead it had a moon painted at the top of the door frame. He smiled at the thought he was entering 'The Moon Room.' The room was not large but it did have its own shower and toilet area for which he was grateful. Since leaving the army he had become accustomed to his own company and feared that being a small hotel he would have to walk down a hall to a bathroom shared by other guests. The bed was a large single, one of those 3 feet 6 inches types. There was a small writing table by the window with a surprisingly modern typing stool. Odd that, bearing in mud the remainder of the furniture was of a vintage style, though very comfortable looking. Jess was well pleased.

CHAPTER THREE

It was now late afternoon.

Looking out from the window he saw what the landlady had mentioned for that is who he assumed she had been. As soon as she had shown him the room she had disappeared back along the corridor. Before him, through the window, was one of those sights of the English countryside that takes your breath away. He could see for miles across wonderful fields of colour, golden browns, beautiful greens. Here and there were fantastic areas and fields of purple linseed plants. The fields were typical of the scene with hardly a square to be seen, all with those hedges so reminiscent of England. There were trees of many varieties, oak, beech, ash, gigantic elms. Far to the right he could see Weeping Willows along a river bank and with the late afternoon sun settling down close to the horizon, it was England as he had never noticed it before.

Unpacking his clothes and setting out his shaving and toiletries, Jess felt as much at home as anywhere he could remember.

It was near to dinner time, though he had not been given any specific or breakfast details, so he decided to have a quick walk around the village green before going back to the hotel for his evening meal. As he strolled along there was so much quiet it was almost deafening, there ought to be people he thought, but could see no one. Passing the pub he noticed a rather overweight black Labrador dog lying fast asleep by the front door. Thinking he might have a drink before going into dinner he stepped past the dog that lazily opened one eye and looked at Jess as if to say, 'Why disturb me?' The eye closed and with a very slight quiver of his tail he seemed to go straight back to sleep.

Opening the pub door and taking a couple of steps inside Jess once more felt he had stepped back in time. Just one bar in a room that could have come straight out of a period so many years in the past it would be difficult to determine its age. The ceilings were low and supported the roof and possible upper floor with huge old beams that had retained their

shape and were all slightly twisted. These were held
in place by further time blackened struts and pillars
in filled with white painted plaster. There were so
many pictures of horses, goats, sheep and assorted
animals along with horse brasses that could have
been hanging there for years without disturbance.
There were etchings, sketches and oil paintings
galore but no gaming machines, no chrome rails or
stained carpet. The floor was old quarry tiles, just
slightly uneven. To Jess it was a superb sight. He
stood there for a moment taking all this in, one
thing struck him immediately. It was the cleanliness
of the place. Years of military life had indoctrinated
him into observing the need for dust free
environments. The inspections of barracks and
getting new recruits into shape meant dust free
rooms and equipment. The floors had to be polished
to a sheen so high that the recruits themselves
would take off their boots and shoes before walking
into the barracks. In those days of service when he
was young the floor was sacrosanct and woe betide
the offender who marked the floor before an
inspection by the sergeant major or duty officer.

The man standing behind the bar counter was portly
and Jess found himself staring at one of the most

prominent red noses he had ever seen. He suddenly became aware that he was staring and had to haul his eyes away from such a dominant proboscis. Yet the face behind that so demanding feature was ruddy and cheerful.

"Lovely afternoon sir. Now can I help you to decide on a refreshing glass of cold cider?"

"Well, yes that would do nicely," Jess replied, just a little surprised that that was exactly what he had in mind. Strange, as normally his preferred tipple was a light beer but the thought about a glass of cider had come to him as he walked through the door. Must be the country atmosphere he thought.

While the landlord drew the cider from a large barrel situated on the counter Jess looked round, taking notice of two very elderly men sitting at a table by the window. They were playing cribbage by the looks of it. There was no conversation between them, just silently dealing and pegging out, playing as if this is all they had ever done from the day of their birth, they being born as old men. If the scene had not been so calming it might have been weird.

A large pint glass filled with a supreme pale amber liquid stood on the counter. It was, he thought, the most rewarding sight he could imagine after his sudden departure from home and the drive to Lower Tumbleford. Taking the first mouthful he allowed it to slide down his gullet with a sensation of perfection, he smiled at the landlord.

"Wonderful."

"Staying at the 'otel are you sir? You won't get better. They will look after you real good."

Jess nodded and said, "Seems a comfortable place to stay, I think I will like it here."

"Staying long then are you?"

"A week or so. It depends on the weather and how good I feel. I want to get some walking in and generally relax."

"Ah, well, if it's walking then you've come to the right place. Lots of places to go to and come back from."

Jess thought about that remark for a moment, it seemed too logical a statement. Did he think I might get lost? So he said to the landlord.

"Are there any areas you would suggest, walks about four or five miles nothing too strenuous. Just easy strolling is what I am anticipating I want to get away from the rat race and forget that the rest of the world exists."

With that the landlord, who was busy behind the counter doing nothing in particular, lurched into a long detailed diatribe of where the best places were and how to get to them. It was so detailed that Jess found himself saying yes and no without remembering half of the instructions. So a good twenty minutes later he finished off his cider, thanked the landlord and left the pub to wander back to the hotel for dinner. Though he had no idea what time that would be. He was half way across the field when he remembered he had not paid for his drink, so back he went and entering the bar with full of apologies asked how much he owed.

"Don't 'e worry about it sir. The 'otel and me have an arrangement, you don't need money to drink here, we will have it put on yer bill over there. Pay when you leave."

To Jess, this seemed an excellent way to do business. In any case he would not want any encouragement to return for more of that superb cider.

CHAPTER FOUR

He returned to the hotel realising that it was now after 6 pm. It appeared that he was the only guest, there being no further tables laid in the small dining area. As he walked in, the woman who earlier on his arrival had introduced herself as May, said that dinner would be ready in about five minutes, so if he wished to avail himself of a sherry on the house, before eating, to please do so. It was on the sideboard. Jess thought about it, but on reflection decided that after a pint of cider, it might spoil his appetite.

There were several old magazines to read and so he picked one about country life and started to read an article about the effects of a certain chemical on the potato crop. Fascinating he thought, I could easily read myself to sleep with that.

True to her word May brought in his meal on an oval plate that should have been described as a salver. It was so large that he thought that it really should have had a Christmas turkey on it. And so was the T-bone steak that took centre spot. This was surrounded by a wonderful variety of vegetables, new peas in butter and French beans. These had a honey coating and when he tasted them they were crisp with an indeterminate flavour which melted away in his mouth. The roast potatoes were done perfectly and there was the finest Sauce Diane.

Then just as he had started eating, May brought in a glass of red wine that had the distinct flavour of a really good Merlot. There was silence as he worked his way through what could only be described as a miracle of cuisine. This triumph was followed after a respectful period, with a most superb trifle which had just the hint of a fine dark sherry. It was a perfect dinner to end a perfect day.

There was just one very small fly in the ointment. How did May know that this was the one meal he loved, with steak done exactly as he would have ordered it. Served with his favourite Sauce Diane and with the one type of wine he preferred above all else then following it with his favourite dessert. On the drive to Tumbleford this is what he had had in mind for dinner. Even then, it was the excellence of the meal that got him looking forward to his stay.

Once she found out that Jess had served with the military and had travelled to so many places in the world, May became quite talkative though mostly about the life he had experienced. He felt rather flattered that she should be so interested and they chattered on till nearly eleven. It was not until much later did he realise that she had told him almost nothing about herself apart from the fact that she had been divorced some years ago and now spent her time running the hotel. The owners were lovely to work for and left her to her own devices with regard to the visitors.

Jess slept the sleep of the innocent and woke the next morning feeling so refreshed and relaxed that going down to breakfast after his morning shave and shower, it was with a little surprise that he found May waiting for him with a King-like English breakfast to end all breakfasts. What a way to start the day he thought and I am waxing poetic into the bargain. Why did I never do something like this before? To just make an immediate decision and act on it to a place like this. But were there many places like Tumbleford? He doubted if there were.

So the next few days went by, a good days walking, a pint or two, of that most drinkable cider, then back to The Tumbleford Hotel for his dinner which had always been of exemplary quality but the content to date had never been repeated. May had continued keeping him company during these meal times and had she missed a turn, he began to believe he would miss her company. The second and third night there had been a couple staying who had kept to themselves, making it plain they did not want to join in any conversations but other than those two, Jess was the only guest. May had served them and was cheerful and attentive enough to them but never talkative with them.

She always came to his table to sit with him during his meal. Jess really liked the companionship and it began to dawn on him that she was a very attractive woman. He began to have the odd slight fantasy about her but each time dismissed the idea as preposterous. It was evident though that May was beginning to be a bit more than just a little friendly towards him and began to intimate perhaps a closer relationship than just being talking companions.

CHAPTER FIVE

It was on the fifth evening after a sumptuous meal, he retired to his room. He settled down with a detective book which was getting so complicated with so many red herrings that he was beginning to doze. Giving up on the novel he decided to have a shower before retiring earlier than normal. It must be the country air he decided with all that walking and so much wonderful food. He finished his shower and was towelling himself dry when there was a gentle knock on the door. He picked up his dressing gown and slipping it over his shoulders went to the door and opened it a few inches, surprising himself with the sight of May standing there. She was wearing what appeared to be a pale blue house coat which had a waist tie that did everything to show the shape of her figure.

"May I come in please Jess?"

For a few seconds Jess was dumbstruck, then gathering his wits he said, "Yes do come in. Funny really because I was just thinking about you."

May stepped into the room and quietly closed the door behind her.

"I thought you might be, somehow I knew we were kindred spirits the moment you first booked in. You stood there looking directly at my chest. I think you did not notice my eyes at all, am I right?"

Jess had spent most of his adult life in the military and was no stranger to sudden changes of tactics in the opposite corner, so it did not take more than a few seconds to adjust to this very pleasant change in his planned evening. He had already decided that he liked May more than normal. It was not love he knew that but being hard was what he was beginning to feel. He had not been with a woman for a long time, not since his wife had departed. A few dates had taken place but he never felt more than casually attracted to any of them and most times his evenings had ended with a good night kiss and many thanks for a lovely time. Vague promises of meeting again sometime but it had never come to pass.

But this felt different. He actually felt excited at the prospect of getting very close to this very attractive female.

May walked over towards him and sitting on the edge of the bed she allowed the front opening of the house coat to drop aside to reveal what Jess had already surmised to be very elegant legs. From where he stood he could glimpse a showing of shiny ice blue panties. She sat on the bed and allowed the housecoat to fall from her shoulders. Smiling at him, she slowly crossed her legs and at the same time managed to lean back which meant that her coat came apart a bit more and his breathing began to quicken when those wonderfully ample breasts came into view.

Jess smiled and slowly walked over to her. He stopped in front of her and without saying a word leant over and softly kissed her on the mouth. The feeling of euphoria at that precise moment was so mind engulfing that his whole body felt as if he was spinning round. He was drunk with the moment. He realising they had all the time in the world to make happen the inevitable. Without uttering a single word, Jess started to slide the housecoat from her shoulders, allowing it to drop onto the floor at her feet. Stepping back a step, he stood there admiring the sight of her so beautiful. She was Aphrodite in proportion and he almost cried out in his adoration. He was so aroused it was painful. May leant forward and pushing his dressing gown off his shoulders, she reached down and gently grasped his manhood. Slipping out of her panties and bra, she stood and wrapped her other hand around his neck. They stood face to face, body to body, chest to breast. The warmth of her body touching his was like being in a warm water shower with all the jets tingling his nerve ends. It was euphoric. He had never experienced this feeling even with his late wife and he had loved her most dearly.

How long they stood there it was impossible to tell. Moving slowly they sunk onto the bed, his hands were travelling across her body exploring, massaging her voluptuous breasts. Kissing her all over, nibbling on her nipples, lowering his head till his lips touched her navel. She tasted so sweet he wanted to keep being with her till Judgment Day. May put her hands each side of his head and without her using any words, he knew what was wanted and now his erection was of immense strength. Gently spreading her legs wide he eased himself into her until he could go no further. Lying there still for a while then slowly, as if on a signal, they both started to gyrate their hips in rotation. Jess knew this was the ultimate sex. This was every man's dream, to make love to a woman in the manner of all his life long dreams put together. Moving as one, they wound and stretched each other's sensations to the limit, the joining so complete that time had no meaning. Sliding effortlessly in and out of her body he was totally infused with his desire and the acceptance May was showing him that he came with so much passion and energy at exactly the moment she was having her own orgasm. It was the climax to end all climaxes. They lay together, still joined as one for a long time, breathing the breath of the totally exhausted.

How long had passed he had no idea, it seemed like it had been hours. He looked at May lying there and still could not believe he had made love to her and that she had reciprocated with such fervour. They were in bed, the absolute couple.

Jess slept, waking as dawn broke through the windows. Rolling over he found he was alone. 'Did I dream all that had gone on,' he wondered. It was so real. Looking around the room there was no evidence that May had ever been there. Deciding he should go steady on the cider, he dressed and went down to breakfast walking into the dining area just as May came in from the kitchen carrying the most wondered plate of eggs, bacon, sausages, fried bread, beans, black sausage and tomatoes. There was also a large pot of freshly made coffee and a most refreshing glass of ice cold orange juice. He was famished.

He looked at her and saw straight into her eyes knowing without any argument that he had not dreamed last night. It had been real. No words were spoken for they both knew that last night had been just the beginning of a wonderful adventure for them both. There was no need for comment or thanks, or words of love, as lovers might. They knew.

CHAPTER SIX

A week had gone by and Jess was walking past the church. It was fairly early in the morning so he was surprised to see this rather angular man wearing a dog collar step out from the church door. Out of politeness Jess gave the vicar a cheery, 'Good morning' and was about to continue his walk when the vicar said,

"I have seen you once or twice walking the roads and bridleways hereabouts. Staying at the hotel are you?"

Jess felt obliged to stop and did so, telling the vicar what a wonderful place it was locally. In fact he almost got carried away with his praise for the village. It was then that the vicar gave a sardonic smile and said,

"You may well think so my friend and I would not gainsay a word against your impression, but be warned, there is more in heaven and earth than meets the eye. Especially to the eye of a stranger to these particular parts."

With that he strode off along a pathway beside the church. It was an overgrown path, to be sure. But the amazing thing was, Jess had not noticed it before and he must have passed the church a dozen times during his walks.

Deciding that if he was to leave this wonderful village of picturesque greens and buildings where he had discovered the most amazing woman of his entire life, then he really must see all the places that the area could offer him. He had a feeling that he was being led down this somewhere road to a valley beyond that would show him fields and hedgerows filled with wild flowers, hedges full of ripe blackberries and small trees where sloes would grow in abundance. He had always enjoyed sloe gin in the mess during his military career.

The Alleyway had given him an insight to the slightly outer properties and their occupants of the village. Though they were more mundane than the centre green with its church and pub.

He thought about that delicious cider. The last mouthful in the glass always gave him a thirst for another.

There was the store that he had not had occasion to visit, having no reason to send postcards or buy groceries. But it seemed nevertheless to have been an integral part of the whole scene. He had looked inside the church but it had appeared pretty normal for a country place of worship, except there did not seem to be any particular branch of religion attached to it.

The whole scene with the village had an air of anticipation and adventure, of thoughts to be hung onto and memories from the past to be regurgitated from the deepest, most dormant recesses of his brain.

CHAPTER SEVEN

Jess walked into the passageway beside the church that same passageway that he had not noticed before his very brief and rather odd conversation with the vicar. What was it the vicar had said?

"There are more things in heaven and earth than meets the eye. Especially in the eye of a stranger in these particular parts."

This thought struck him as he entered the passageway. It was overgrown and had not been tended for many years, which was another thought that crept through his mind. Still the vicar had just walked through as if it had been totally clear of all the overhanging branches and foliage. The vicar's comment which had seemed so innocuous at the time kept coming back to him as he struggled on past all the tangle of creepers. He was clearly reminded of some of the jungle in faraway places that he had forced his way through with machete in one hand and an automatic in the other. It was a strange way to leave a pathway after a total neatness of the village.

It must have been a good half hour before it began to thin out.

'Where has the vicar gone?' he wondered. Still he had come this far along the pathway so might as well try to see where it went to.

Suddenly without even a single step forward he was out in the open. He had pushed aside a curtain of large leaf strands and there he was at the beginning and in the centre of a large road way. It stretched before him for miles without end, disappearing into the distance to a finite point on the horizon. Little did Jess know at that time but he had arrived at the ultimate destination that fate had decreed he should experience, before the rest of his life began.

CHAPTER EIGHT

Jess stood there for a few minutes, just staring. He knew from all his experience in the military that had this road existed he would have seen it on his walks. Yet here it was, long and straight and bordered by huge elm trees on either side. These were all in the stages of dropping leaves as they would in late autumn. That cannot be right for when he entered the passageway it was high summer. Everything had been in full bloom and it had had the warmth of beautiful summer days. Here it was chilly and he gave a small shiver. He wondered if it was because the temperature was lower or because the scene laid out before him gave off a sinister sensation of long forgotten dangers.

It made no difference to his automatic decision to walk on down The Road.

So began his trip of times past.

Waking slowly he allowed his gaze to wander over the scenario before him. The trees were spaced about thirty yards apart and were all of a standard height, similar to a garden privet hedge but standing some fifty feet tall. Around the base of them all and as far as he could see there were a mixtures of wild flowers, dandelions, ragwort, daises, cowslips, dog roses and nettles and deadly nightshade. These all grew among bushes of a number of varieties such as Holly, rosehip, wild clematis in many different shades of green, red, yellow, purple mixed in a jumble of colour, shape and texture. Jess was no horticulturist but was still surprised they could all survive in what seemed like a miniature jungle.

The word jungle penetrated his thoughts and he started to recall some of his life prior to his years in the army, times as a boy when growing up he and his mates fought mock battles. There were always arguments about who would be the enemy because the enemy had to lose in any war of their imagination.

His thoughts went to when he was about ten years old with Billy Johnson, Brian Slope, Terry Parker and Trevor Cottrill who had come across a group of like youngsters from an adjacent street. There had always been animosity between the two streets.

Where Jess lived it was the only privately owned street of houses in the town, so the tenants from the council and other rented properties considered Jess and his mates as the posh kids from The Drive. It wasn't that he lived in a big house, quite the opposite. Many of the tenant and council houses were larger and boasted bigger gardens. No, it was the mere fact of people actually owning their own house that gave the other kids, what Jess later in life surmised was an inferiority complex. It didn't matter though, he and his mates were classed as the posh kids.

On this particular day it was evident that the others wanted some sort of confrontation, so they started to hurl insults about Jess and his friends being yellow bellies, cowardly custards and other names that were in vogue at that time. After a few minutes tempers got the better of them and one of his mates, he thought it might have been Billy, picked up a stone and threw it in the direction of the other group. This unfittingly encouraged the others to retaliate which they did and soon stones were flying between them, albeit that most were landing short, doing no harm whatsoever. But suddenly Terry cried out and looking round Jess saw that Terry was bleeding badly from the mouth. One stone had been thrown just that bit more and it had struck home, right on Terry's mouth. It was obvious that something untoward had happened and when the other group saw the blood had been spilled they just turned and scarpered back to their own street.

This incident tended to stop that type of exchange between the two groups but there was always tension and several individual fights at the school they all attended.

It was one of these minor altercations that Jess himself got involved in. As he continued his walk along The Road, he began to wonder why he was thinking about all those days so long in the past but think about them he did, he found that despite trying not to his mind kept falling back to memories he thought he had long forgotten.

The fight with the other boy came not from one of the normal group of childish enemies but a new kid. He didn't know it then but later in life he had reason to know his name very well indeed. A lad of the same age as Jess but a fraction taller, blonde and rather fair skinned with an angelic face and bright blue eyes. As Jess remembered that it must have been him who started the fracas, telling the other lad he looked rather girly. At first there was no response but after some extra baiting the other boy had said,

"Pack it in. I'm not calling you names, so why are you having a go at me?"

Naturally this was an invitation for some of the other boys to start in with their six pennyworth and before many seconds had gone by there was a call, as there always was, for a fight. As Jess had started the whole business it was considered playground honour for him to be the chosen one. Walking forward he pushed the new boy in the chest causing him to stagger back a few paces but he recovered quicker than Jess had imagined he would. Before Jess could understand what had happened, he was flat on his back with the new boy astride him and turning his arm to the point of pain but not quite breaking it.

"I told you to pack it in," he said. "I do not want to fight you but if you keep it up I will give you a good hiding you won't forget."

With that he got off Jess's chest and started to walk away across the playground. By this time all of the friends that Jess thought he had were also getting some distance from the pair of them. He felt bitter that he had allowed a complete stranger to fell him so easily, at the same time not really knowing how it had been done. What he did do was to ask himself the question, 'If that other boy could knock me down so effortlessly without actually striking a blow, then I must find out his secret.'

He decided then and there to swallow his pride and simply ask him. It was the following day when he found himself in line with the other boy who was avoiding looking at him. So with the bravado that would later stand him in good stead he said,

"My name's Johnathon, everyone calls me Jess, because of my initials J.E.S.S. Got to admit you caught me yesterday, how did you do that?"

"Jujitsu. It's a type of martial art. My name's Hardy Grimes. Everyone calls me Hardy strange as it may seem."

CHAPTER NINE

It seemed just then that a bond sprang up between them that would last till that terrible day many years later that Jess would never ever forget. It would nag at him for the rest of his life. Could he have done more to save the life of the truest friend he had.

His mind jumped forward to that day twenty years later when they were in the same group that had been directed to infiltrate the enemy lines in order to bring out a senior officer who had been captured by the enemy. This particular officer held staff rank and was privileged to information that would help the enemy in quite a big way. He had used his rank to go up front. As a result of his inexperience in this sector he and his clerk sergeant had been isolated and picked up by an enemy patrol. They were now in one of the camps awaiting removal to an intelligence section. So getting back was very important and it had to be done as quickly as possible before they realised just who they had in captivity. So it was that Jess and his small group, which included Hardy Grimes of Jess school days, had been allocated the task of retrieval.

Jess really did not want to think about that day but The Road kept reminding him. As he glanced sideways it seemed that the trees were no longer stout elms but large red trees and the weeds were scraggy undergrowth that was almost impenetrable. He was remembering only too well.

They had gone out in the early hours, just five of them, all part of one unit that was officially unofficial. A blind eye was turned as to their methods as long as they were successful and did not allow themselves to be caught and interrogated. He remembered the induction into this unit following time spent in the SAS. He was told that he could leave and go back to his own infantry regiment or he could stay and forever be anonymous in the military field of warfare. In other words he would not exist should he be captured. He would never be able to tell anyone about his military life. He would to all intents and purposes be an ordinary member of one of the lesser renowned infantry regiments. Acceptance did not seem an option to Jess at that time and so started his new life as an unknown soldier He sported the rank of captain and was given the odd title of Inspecting Ground Officer. This gave him and a few others like him the ability to move around without any specific duties. Any reports he made were coded and submitted to a ministry of defence official of staff rank in the forces who was just called 'The Boss.'

His own little group had been called in to carry out this particular task. There were very severe political and military problems attached should anything go wrong and on this occasion it did. In every well planned journey there is always that tiny element of good luck or bad luck that is needed for success or failure.

They had been dropped early dawn into an area some two miles behind the lines where intelligence was certain that no enemy traffic had been reported for some days. So it was in every respect a good landing point to start their sortie.

All had gone well, all five of them landed and stowed their chutes in the brush where they would not be found for a long time, if ever. Armed with machine pistols, knives and other weapons of their choice, which included if required, hypodermic syringes to put any opposing soldier down quietly and manageable. This would give the impression later that he had just gone to sleep on duty. Much better than loads of blood and dead bodies left lying around.

Everything was going as planned and after daylight arrived they settled down to wait till the next evening when they could infiltrate the outskirts of the camp where they were informed the captive officer was being held.

Towards dusk they got ready to move over the last mile of terrain. It was brush and small trees from a few inches to ten or twelve feet in height. Their problem was that it had been cleared all around the perimeter for about a hundred yards and it was that hundred yards that had prevented them from making their insurgence during daylight. Now it was getting dark, this had to be done before the moon came out. There were some boulders around and it was these that afforded them some vestige of cover as they crawled forward.

The entrance as such was no more than a gap and was guarded by two soldiers who thought that being some distance from the front they were reasonably safe and so were not as vigilant as they should have been. They did not see Jess and his team advance to a section of the perimeter that was just out of their sight. Cutting through the wire just enough to afford entry they wriggled through and silently made for the area that probably housed the senior officers. From there it was hoped that any captives would be held. After some moments waiting they observed food in large tins being taken to an enclosure just a hundred yards or so from where they were hiding. As they watched a troop of soldiers paraded and then went out via the entrance for the nights patrol.

Once it had quietened down enough to assume that most of the inmates were having their evening meal Jess motioned for them to approach the hut where the tins of food had been taken. Signalling that they were to stay there and give him covering fire if required he slowly started to walk towards the hut. His clothing had been taken long ago from other prisoners so his presence would not attract too much attention as long as he did not encounter anyone who might feel inclined to challenge him as to why he was so near that particular hut.

It was going well so far and when he was next to the wall of the hut he managed to find a small crack in the wall through which he could see some of the interior. Though he did not have a view of the whole room nor could he see the officer they were after. But he was aware that there was someone there from movement noise. He hoped that the officer was there and that he would understand the word 'JESS'.

He lightly tapped on the wooden slats the hut was made from. The movement noise stopped and after a few moments there was an answering few taps. Then a voice speaking as if to itself said,

"How the hell did I get myself in this mess?"

Then silence. Jess tapped again in Morse. 'We can help.' Then a face appeared in view from the gap which Jess could see through.

Jess said, "Start singing, not loudly but as if you were trying to keep your spirits up."

There came a soft tenor voice singing a Gilbert and Sullivan piece about the constabulary. It was enough for Jess to insert a small lever into one of the slats to see how firmly they were fixed. He couldn't believe his luck as the first one came off without a sound. Continuing he was able to loosen three more. He didn't pull them right off. Just enough so that when the time came he would be able to take them off quickly and replace them enough so that it would not be immediately noticeable.

Then he said, "We will be back as soon as the camp has bedded down for the night."

With that he sauntered away and managed to disappear into the area where there were no significant lighting and where his team had managed to hide amongst empty crates and old fuel drums.

Keeping still and quiet for the next few hours had been part of their very extensive training so with the mental attitude of the very patient they settled down and waited. It was some three hours later that Jess deemed it safe to emerge and go over to the back of the hut where the loose boards were. Tapping quietly he heard a minute tap back in acknowledgement. Slowly and carefully removing each board he had previously loosened he opened a gap enough for the officer inside to squeeze through. Here the first of those unlucky breaks came to the fire. They had taken away his boots and socks so he was barefoot. It could not be rectified so off they went back through the hole in the wire and crawled away as quietly as possible with an officer who was without, boots, shoes and even socks.

They had some three miles to cover before they could reach their own lines. It was at times like this that your own side may not really believe who you are and start shooting. But his team had done all this before and were usually successful in avoiding the shooting part, even though they had sometimes spent a night in a British front line military jail before all was cleared.

It had been slower going than they had hoped. They had to stop long enough to wrap the staff officer's feet so that he was able to trek back along the lines. Hardy was in the lead, taking as much care as time would allow. They had reached a point some four hundred yards from their own lines when several shots rang out from behind them. There was no time for too much care and they started to hurry but suddenly he had fallen. He had been shot in the lower right of his back and could not move. Their escape had been detected and a patrol sent out after them. The slower staff officer's lack of foot covering had slowed them enough for the enemy's patrol to catch up within firing range but they were still six hundred yards behind Jess and his team. The shot that had hit Hardy was a fluke shot. Carrying Hardy between them, they hurried forwards to their own lines where by now there was covering fire which had stopped the followers from coming any closer.

That night, Hardy died.

CHAPTER TEN

Jess found himself crying as he walked along The Road. So many bad memories. He had always felt himself to blame as he had insisted that Hardy had to be one of his team that night and by his insistence he had got Hardy killed. Jess knew better really but had never been able to shrug off that feeling of guilt.

It had been Hardy who was selected first for the special duties team and had recommended Jess. After the preliminary training they had worked well together and had been on many sorties as part of each other's teams but the guilt was still there and would never go away.

Jess began to feel the rain and thought perhaps he should retrace his steps back to the village. How long he had been walking he had no idea. As he looked back he couldn't see the start of the road he was on, it seemed to disappear over the brow of the rise in the surface. He couldn't even see the top of the church but started to trek his way back to the village the way he had come. There was no alternative as there were no turnings off. He started to day dream again.

The Road had not quite finished with Johnathon Edward Spencer-Smith.

As deeply affected as he was by the death of his closest friend Hardy Grimes, he was still very much aware of all the better times there had been in his life. Looking back at his marriage, he could clearly remember meeting his ex-wife for the first time. In those days he did not have a car, so it was either walk or catch the bus to get anywhere. On that particular evening he had been to the cinema alone and coming out after the film had ended he had found that it was as usual raining. Not hard but that incessant drizzle that soaked you to the skin, no matter how good your clothing. She seemed to be pretty of face with fair hair hanging long to her shoulders. About five feet tall and slim, he guessed her age at around twenty two or thereabout. Jess was not in uniform, as his kind of duties required a certain anonymity but he had a ready smile and a countenance that tended to promote comfort and safety.

Smiling he said,

"Have you been waiting long? I rather thought there was a bus due about this time."

"I've only been a few minutes. I do so hope that I won't have to wait long. I seem to be soaked through already."

Standing there, Jess thought what a really lovely face she had, not the classic beauty but pretty and comfortable. He felt he ought to know this girl better and so with that easy way he had with anyone he met, or indeed needed to know, he decided to keep the conversation going.

"I suppose as usual it has either gone through early or it will be fifteen minutes late. They have time tables printed but don't seem to be able to keep to them."

She smiled again and to Jess it seemed she wanted the conversation to carry on. Perhaps she feels safer with me than with the unknown, he thought but was a little put out by her next remark.

"I have seen you around the town a couple of times, always on your own. I thought at first that you were the army but they always wear uniform. What do you do?"

Jess thought for a moment before replying. He didn't want to lie but could not tell the whole truth, so with a big grin on his face he said,

"Well it's like this. I am in the army but when I joined I insisted they get me a uniform that was tailored to fit me proper and though they kept trying they just haven't managed to find a tailor who is good enough for me so I have to keep wearing civilian clothes till they do."

Laughing at his little joke they continued chatting till the bus came along ten minutes later. Jess found it was a natural thing for him to sit next to her and surprisingly enough when she rose to get off he jumped up too and stepped off with her.

"Thought I would walk you home if you agree."

Saying nothing she looped her arm in his and off they went. He gave her a simple kiss on the forehead as they parted, having arranged to meet again in a few days. So it was after some six months and numerous stays at various hotels that they decided to get married. Jess had often wondered since then if it was his rank as captain that had persuaded her into the matrimonial state. It had certainly been a bone of contention, for as time went by and he was not promoted she began to moan about his lack of ambition. Why did so-and-so get made up to major and above and you have stayed as a captain. He tried to explain but he could not tell her the truth about his kind of duties. Especially when he was away, often for weeks at a time and would not, could not, tell her where he had been or what he had been doing. As time progressed into their marriage, tension entered every time he went off on one of his jaunts, as she would phrase it.

Returning home became a trial of arguments and stress for them both. So as the years went by they began to tolerate each other and he guessed that she had lovers though he always chose to ignore the fact. Eventually though it had come to a head when he arrived home several days ahead of schedule to find her entangled in the sheets and another man's body.

He had stood in the entrance to the bedroom then walked over stripped the sheets from the bed, grabbed the other man by the arm and frog marched him to the front door and shoved him out into the street totally naked. To this day he had no idea where the man had gone or who he had been. Then taking suitcase from the cupboard he told her to fill it with her clothes and get out. Looking back he was surprised that she had done so. He had called a taxi for her and directed the driver to a hotel in town. At the time it had all seemed so easy, just being quiet and outwardly calm, decisive to the point of military operation. It had worked then but had she argued, or shouted, or gone into one of her usual verbal ravings he was not sure how it would have turned out. At the time it was the right thing for him to. The divorce went through quietly and without too much fuss and there had been a few times when he had the notion that there had been some behind the scenes negotiations that he was not aware of. He said nothing in order to prevent any undue publication about his line of work within the military. It did not matter now.

Slowly walking on down The Road he wondered whether all the times he had put his life on the line for his country had made any difference. Had the several times he had killed, both from a distance and at very close quarters, been effective in creating a better world? Being told it was essential; to remove a certain person from this life was a good thing in the long run and had been his life. It was no use mulling over the rights and wrongs of such doings. They were done and time cannot be turned back. His thoughts were churning over in his mind like ballast in a mixer, nothing tangible now, all bits and pieces. Memories were tumbling about. His first time making love to his ex-wife it had been so well arranged. They had gone to a hotel at the coast, trying to appear casual to the receptionist and all the time thinking about her naked body against his. His first thrust of passion, the climaxing together, three, four, five times he had entered her that night, so long ago and now with such bitter memories.

His mind raced on to his first kill. It had been a soldier on guard duty, just a soldier on guard. He may have been married with children, though he did seem too young for that. But as the very sharp knife had sliced across his throat, the lad had given a slight gurgle and slid to the ground. There he was left to whatever military funeral his compatriots would give him.

After that Jess had a few dreams to remind him of his deed but that is what war is about. After the second and third time it began to numb his mind to the true horror of his actions. It was war and war made killers out of many, either by design as in Jess's case or by accident when shooting a gun from a distance might, or might not, kill or injure someone.

Jumbled thoughts, regrets, good times and bad were all that Jess could get his mind onto. Above all there was one thing that kept his feet stepping forward, he wanted to get out of this Road. It was too painful now. He kept images of May back at the Hotel and the warm comfort of her arms and body. Her lovemaking was for the past week, all that he could have wished for.

As more thoughts of May came into his head, he gradually became aware that he was back at the beginning of The Road. He scrambled back along the pathway and into the cosiness of the village green. Striding straight to the pub he found much to his amazement, that it was closed. Cutting across the green he went into the entrance of the hotel at the side and was met by a rather stern man in his fifties who greeted him saying,

"Good evening sir. You have had a good stay and plenty of interesting walks. I am expecting you'll want your bill as you're leaving early. I will get your breakfast as usual. Be glad when the wife gets back from her sisters in London, been gone two weeks now she has."

Jess looked at him and said, "I'd like to speak to May if she's about."

The landlord, who Jess guessed he was, looked at him in a rather odd way before saying quietly, "Yes sir, I daresay you would but then so would many others who have stayed here. May has not lived here for over a hundred and fifty years."

THE THIEF

CHAPTER ONE

Sarah Pickering at twenty nine was a slim, fair haired woman with an athletic figure. She was the sort of woman to whom men would give more than a second glance. Her long wavy hair appeared almost golden in certain lights and framed her striking face. Even then, she could appear haughty and unfriendly to those who did not know her.

A stranger who knew not of her upbringing, might assume she was from a well-heeled family used to comfort and the good things in life. They may assume she had loving parents and a happy and healthy family environment.

It would have come as a shock to know the truth.

Arthur 'Sap' Pickering, Sarah's father, was a boozer. He liked several pints every day and although not a drunkard, was known to get drunk fairly often. When he was drunk, he could become violent and this was one of the many reasons that Sarah learnt at an early age to keep well clear of him. He had never hit Sarah, instead choosing to take his temper out on her mother.

At five foot ten inches tall, he was of a slim build and wiry which caused the muscles to stand out on his arms like strips of thick rope. This combination of wiry strength and height made him a formidable opponent in the numerous scraps he managed to get himself into.

Born in Dagenham in 1955 he began his working life at the Ford plant. His father and uncle had put in a good word for him to ensure he was given a job there. It was considered a good start for a young lad just leaving school who had only just scraped through his lessons and had no written qualifications.

The problems started after the first couple of years when he became bored and argumentative with those in authority and in particular his immediate foreman. He was often late for work and started taking sick leave for two and three days at a time, mainly after drinking too much the night before. Eventually a very serious argument arose between himself and the foreman, culminating in 'Sap' threatening to carve him with a Stanley knife. It was the interference of other workers that prevented it happening. The result was that he was dismissed. No charges were brought. He was now foot loose and fancy free but with no wages.

His own father would have given him a good bashing but Sap was now getting as tall and as strong as his father so once again he walked away from any undue punishment.

It was while on one of his wanderings around the town that he saw the recruitment centre for the army. Out of curiosity he went in and listened to the recruiting sergeant who explained what a wonderful life he would lead as a soldier with the chance of promotion and regular hours. It all sounded far too good to miss and he was bored. He signed on for five years.

He found that life as a soldier was as good as anything that he had had before and certainly better than he would get as a civilian. He drifted into the life and signed on for the full tour. Though a good soldier in a fight, he always managed to get into trouble with those senior to him. This prevented any promotions that he might have expected. It was the Falklands War that brought it all to a head. He was getting older and though somehow he had never shirked from a fight he found it was too much. After the first few weeks he was shipped home and retired on an army disability pension. He later used the concept of Post-Traumatic Stress Disorder to cover for his many brushes with the law and his own mates, his wife and daughter.

After the Falklands War, he was fit only for labouring and a sometime lorry driver for companies who were more interested in the arrival of their indistinct cargo than the sobriety and uprightness of their staff. On these jobs he was often away from home for three days at a time and this gave his long suffering wife plenty of opportunity to have her men friends around.

And of them there were many.

As a young teenager, Sarah came to dread the boyfriend visits as much as she dreaded her father returning from work. Her father would shout and threaten violence, there had been the few occasions when had ripped up her homework and one time when he had urinated all over it in front of her. Her school had not understood this and it had caused her to get admonished by the teachers. Her mother's boyfriends would touch and often stroke her arms and thighs. But her mother would threaten her with violence if she said anything while at the same time often giving her money as bribes. Sarah learnt to keep out of the way.

For these reasons, Sarah learnt to trust no one.

One afternoon when she had returned from school and was doing her home work in the unusually peaceful kitchen, the doorbell rang. She ignored it initially but the persistent melody of, 'Yes we have no bananas,' forced her to slam down her pen on the kitchen table and go and answer it.

"Where's yer mam?" asked the obviously drunk and dishevelled man leaning forward in the porch way.

"She's at work."

"And yer dad?"

"He's away."

As soon as the words were out of her mouth, she realised her mistake. The man, whom she vaguely remembered as Tom or Dick or something, pushed his way inside and shut the door behind him.

"So it's just us two is it?"

"I have a friend coming over any minute now, so I should leave if I were you."

"You aint got no friends. Yer mother told me. No one's coming over, so stop lying to me."

He sat on the sofa and patted the seat next to him, "Come and sit next to me."

Sarah tensed and began walking towards the front door. For a drunk, Tom Perry was quick on his feet and he beat her to it. He locked the door, took the key and gave her a heavy slap across the face. While an assault such as this might have upset the equilibrium of a normal teenager, Sarah was unfazed. She picked up an umbrella and hit him across the neck and then used the pointy end to jab him firmly in the gut.

He punched her and then knocked her sideways onto the sofa. Before she could regain her senses, he was on top of her and began ripping open her school blouse. Sarah was too stunned to resist and by the time she realised what was happening, her skirt was up around her waist and her blouse wide open.

By now Tom was aroused to the point where his thinking was not sensible. All he could see in his drunken mind was a particularly luscious body that needed all he could give it.

Grabbing her hands in a vice like grip of his one hand, he held them above her head and with his other hand tore off her knickers. He bent and sucked on her breasts and she felt he was almost biting them, she struggled. Oh how she struggled but he was far too strong for her.

His hand went down to her crotch and he started to finger her roughly, then she felt his engorged penis pushing against her, trying to force himself inside. At last his efforts managed to do just that and with a hard push he rammed himself inside her. She felt the pain and the final shove that meant that no more was she a virgin. She was in agony but as he pushed into her his grip on her hands relaxed and she got one hand free.

It was as her arm came down to try to get him off her that her fingers touched the scissors her mother always kept under one of the cushions on the settee. They were sharp pointed and with supreme effort of will she brought them out with an upward motion. Then with a downward strike she rammed them into his buttock. She again wrenched them free and jammed them into his thigh.

Tom screamed and rolled off her onto the floor yelling,

"What the bloody hell have you done?"

But his injuries were too painful for him to stop Sarah scrambling to her feet and dashing upstairs to her small bedroom. Once there she slammed the door and locked it tight, pushing as much furniture as she could against the door. She stayed there for some time till she heard the back door slam. She felt degraded and totally humiliated. She hated Tom Perry with a passion that was beyond emotion. Over the next few minutes it generated into an obsession that all men were animals and she would exact revenge on as many as she could. Hate was her forte and it was to drive her onward for many years to come.

She was certain he had not climaxed inside her. When her mother was writhing on the sofa with one of her boyfriends, Sarah had watched sometimes from a crack in the door and had some idea what to expect. Nevertheless as soon as she felt safe she went to the bathroom and washed herself as much as possible. There had been some blood but it was not as bad as she thought and so she was able to tidy herself up before her mother came home.

Though a promiscuous woman, she was still a mother and it did not take many moments for her to realise that something was wrong with her daughter. A few penetrating questions brought out the truth.

So it was that her father was told who had raped his daughter. Such information was not for the likes of the police and the local papers to dramatise but Tom Perry was never seen again. Some folks rumoured that he had been found drowned in the mud of the Thames near Tower Bridge. It was never confirmed nor denied.

CHAPTER TWO

Family life remained pretty much the same with her father going away intermittently on his driving runs and her mother bringing home boyfriends following her trips to the pub.

Sarah just got on with her studies, staying at her gran's every so often and stealing money from her mum's purse when she needed fags or new clothes. Her mother didn't punish her, favouring her silence over her misdemeanours.

The memories of her rape stayed with her and continued to fester. She had grown into a very attractive girl and many of the boys at her school found that her attitude towards the male strange. So the rumour grew that she was more lesbian than straight. Sarah did nothing to disprove this but she began to understand that her looks were the one big advantage she had in life. Her standards at school were quite good, though not in the top five percent.

University was not an option. Even had she the required standards, her home life could not have sustained her so it was that finding a job after school was necessary. After several interviews she was offered a post with an advertising agency, giving her the opportunity to meet other people of her own age and older. It was the older generation of men that thought she would be a pushover for sex.

Her first encounter in this field was the office manager, a thirty year old, not badly turned out, both from looks and in his attire. He asked her out and she agreed but decided that it would be on her terms. She told him she would meet him in the bar of a respectable hotel nearby, guessing that he would probably book a room on the strength of her choice of location. So it was that after a couple of drinks with a good dinner he invited her up to his room. Once there, he opened another bottle of wine and held out a glass for her. Sarah refused, asking with a very innocent look why he had wanted to bring her to his room.

He said,

"Come on Honey, surely you are not that shy. I thought we had an understanding?"

"Oh! I think we understand alright but will your wife agree?"

With that she turned and walked out the door.

It did not take long for her to extract certain favours from him that helped her progress through the system and along with that progress came the chance to meet more influential clients. She began to be offered money to keep quiet about her meetings with some of these men. Never getting to the point of going to bed with them she did allow some fondling in order to gain the advantage. Then would come the gentle art of extracting money, clothing and often jewellery.

Finding out about the men she met before encouraging them to ask her out became a habit and the more she discovered about certain fetishes of many of them, the more she was able to squeeze out of them. Her activities in this field expanded to those men who really preferred bondage as part of their sexual turn-on. This was just what Sarah had been unconsciously aiming for, to punish men and not have to deal with the problem of sleeping with them.

So began a period of her life that incorporated the whips, handcuffs and other assorted items of applying pain to men. Having to dress in various dress styles was a small part to play in order to satisfy her desire to punish all men for her rape. This continued for a good few years till she was in her late twenties. She was a striking woman whose list of clients considered themselves lucky to be her slave as and when required.

The problems started when she was approached by one of her clients who suggested that she form an alliance with him and a few of his friends. The suggestion was broached in such a manner that it was in effect a threat.

"Let us in on your deal or we will make sure your looks do not last for too much longer."

After some considerable thought as to how best overcome the threat, Sarah reached the conclusion that the threat was not an idle one. She had two options. Go in with them or get out of the business altogether. Neither was what she wanted but getting out was the best answer as she would no longer be able to lead her own life but would be the 'employee' of a group of 'employers' of the West End criminal fraternity and that did not fit in with her idea of life in any way.

But how to get out? These were nasty people who would not take a 'No thank you.' easily.

Sarah had by common sense built up a decent financial portfolio. She had not over spent and had accumulated a fair amount worth she estimated, to be in the region of close to £900,000 or so. Certainly enough to live comfortably till other opportunities came along.

She decided to give up her flat and perhaps go abroad for a while. It was a good flat in a good position, so she had no bother finding a new tenant. It was while she was packing that she came across an advert that simply said,

If you want a quiet place to stay

Then why not enjoy the comforts

Of a discreet hotel with home cooking.

The Tumbleford Hotel.

Tumbleford.

The Midlands.

What it was about the advert she did not understand, but it seemed just right. This was how she found herself driving her Mazda sports saloon on the main M1 going north. Why she had not thought to get more instruction as to the route, she never did recall but not far past Nottingham she saw a small sign leading off a slip road that just read Tumbleford.

The turning led into a country road with almost no traffic which after several more turns of direction became a single track lane. This lane felt like it would go on for ever but just as Sarah was beginning to despair of her rash impulse on such a simple advert, the lane passed some heavy roadside foliage and came out into a village where a sign read.

Welcome to Tumbleford.

CHAPTER THREE

As a city born and bred girl, Sarah had tended to holiday in cities. Even when she travelled abroad it had always been to large population areas and coastal towns and popular holiday centres, so her concept of what a country village should be was perhaps much like Tumbleford. A large grassed area surrounded by a roadway which in turn was lined with properties. These all faced towards the green, all different in style and age. There was a church, a store come shop with a post office. There was the Inn and almost directly opposite there appeared a building larger than the rest with a sign stating that it was The Tumbleford Hotel.

On first impressions it had maybe four to six visitor rooms with enough other rooms for the owner's private accommodation. But oddly, there did not seem to be a front entrance. This scene was taken in at first glance as Sarah stopped at the junction and gave a quick survey of the place.

"What have I let myself in for?" she wondered. Still it certainly was isolated and perhaps this will be that 'away from it all' location that she so badly needed in order to get herself in tune with her new situation.

More than ever as she had driven along, her thoughts had moved along the lines that perhaps it was a sign that she should get out of the business of bondage and if possible start something more respectable. But just what could she do? Or where?

Driving around the central green she came to the hotel, noticing at this point that there was a side door entrance to the left of the front. Leaving her car outside, she walked to the entrance and pushed open the door. The reception, for that was what lay beyond the door she had just opened, was quite small, perhaps just large enough for three or four people to stand. Sarah found herself wondering why all small hotel lobbies and reception areas were much the same wherever she had travelled. There was a hatchway with a pay phone on its shelf, a small table with a clutter of brochures, some small potted plants that always needed watering and the inevitable small hand bell to summon the attending clerk. This was however different, the paintwork was a delicate cream and cheerful looking, the carpet on the floor was a luxurious chocolate brown. It all exuded comfort and wellbeing.

She rang the hand bell.

She did not notice the door open or hear the person who she now found standing next to her. She suddenly became aware that she was not alone and as she slowly turned, for some reason was rooted to the spot without a word to say.

For the first time since she was fifteen here stood a man about her own age who was not repulsive to her. She felt herself drawn to him like a bee to honey.

He said, "Let me guess, you would like a room for a few nights and you do not want anyone outside the village to know you are here. Though of course this being a village, they already do know but you can be certain it will be kept very, very secret."

With that he smiled. He smiled the smile of the sincere on a face that was if anything, a rugged face. It had the look of someone who spent a good deal of his time outdoors, clean shaven with a mop of light wavy brown hair that tended to slide forward onto his brow. Most of all were his eyes that were a piercing blue which Sarah knew could look into her innermost thoughts and not judge her at all. Standing at about six feet with an athletic build, he was wearing dark brown corduroy trousers, a check shirt and a deep red open neck jumper. She had no idea about his footwear as she was standing too close to see without being rude, yet she could not remember ever wanting to stand this close to any man before. She started to calm herself because she had the strangest feeling that she wanted to stand even closer.

"Yes please, that would be nice," she heard herself saying. "I do not really know how long I will be here."

"That's really OK. Stay as long as you wish, I am sure you will find everything you are looking for. I will show you to your room. My father has allocated you room five. It's called the Sunflower Room and overlooks the fields at the back. You will like it, there is no traffic noise."

With that he gave a little chortle. It was an infectious laugh that had Sarah grinning like a cat after a dish of cream.

Walking back through the door he had recently come from he said,

"Please follow me .I will show you the room and get your luggage from your car. Your car can be left at the side of the hotel, till you need it. But I think you may not need it at all while you are staying here."

Following him up the stairs she found herself along a fairly wide hallway with just six doors leading off. Reaching the end he opened the door for her and while doing so said,

"My name is Keith, Miss Pickering. We start serving dinner at six pm but come down whenever you feel comfortable. Your bags are there on the side table, if you wish for anything to drink there is tea and coffee in the small cupboard to the left of the television."

With that he was gone, leaving Sarah wondering just how he was involved in her reason for being here and how the blazes he had known her name.

However, the room was nicely decorated in a comfortable cream and light brown. The carpets appeared new and unworn. The room was a decent size with a queen size bed, side tables, a separate table and dining chair plus a deep red upholstered arm chair that looked as if it would be a sensation to sit in.

Then she noticed in the corner another door which when opened gave access to a wonderful en-suite bathroom with shower and all other amenities. There were soaps and shampoos, conditioners and incredibly large bath towels. These were all the little things that you would only get in the most expensive of establishments.

"I think I will like it here," she mused.

Then deciding to test it all, she had a shower that was as good as it promised. The towels were as perfect as those in her own flat, the oils and creams supplied were so nice on her skin she felt if anything a little aroused by the surprise of it all. Making herself a coffee from the various brands available, she drank while dressing.

'Someone must have brought my luggage up while I was showering,' she thought. 'I didn't hear them come in or open the drawers to the dresser. They must have been very quiet to lay out everything so neatly in the drawers as only a woman could do.'

Dressing in a pale blue two piece and noticing the time was now just after six thirty, she walked back down the stairs and found the dining room off to the right. Entering, she was again surprised by the quality of all the furnishings and the table layout, really high quality silver. There were just two other apparent residents, an old couple who looked and smiled then got on with their dinner.

As she sat down, Keith came in and offered her the menu.

"You will find everything on the menu is available. I highly recommend the lamb and if I may be so bold, I would like to say how lovely you look. The blue really suits your skin tone."

Sarah was a little taken aback but pleased that he should notice and be honest enough to comment.

"That's very nice of you to say so. I will have the lamb then."

"Good. You will be well pleased with your choice. I hope your things were arranged as you would wish, I was not too certain on some items."

Sarah suddenly realised that he had been arranging her clothes in the drawer and wardrobe while she was in the shower. Blushing deeply she said as matter of fact as possible.

"It was very kind of you to do so and yes it was just as I would have wished."

Somehow it felt perfectly reasonable that a complete stranger would be handling her rather expensive underwear and a man at that. She felt no qualms about him having done so and a little thrill crept down her spine at the thought.

Sarah decided not to have any starter as she found often that it ruined her appetite for the main course and somehow she had an inkling that the main was to be a triumph. The lamb was incredible, succulent and free of fat. The vegetables, carrots and parsnips were cut in about one inch sticks and cooked in sweet water and butter. The roast potatoes were done to perfection and all served in a delicate mint sauce. She had a passion for red wines and disregarded convention, so chose a very nice Australian Merlot from the Barossa Valley area.

As a dessert, she thought a good old fashioned steamed chocolate pudding with light flavoured custard was in order. Her choice was perfect and it was a meal that could not have been better cooked or presented by the finest chef in the western world. Keith had been her waiter all through the meal and had made no more than a few remarks about her choice of meal. This had pleased her for having eaten for many years alone in the comfort of her own home she did not respond well with too much chatter at the meal table.

As she relaxed after such a delicious repast and started thinking about a nice coffee, Keith said,

"I trust you enjoyed your meal Miss Pickering, perhaps a coffee would make a good finish."

"Oh! Yes please Keith, that would be wonderful, maybe something with a Grand Marnier liqueur."

"Easily arranged Miss, we stock most drinks. It's a proud boast that we have never been asked for a drink that we cannot provide. There are some foods that we would not stock, for example Kangaroo meat, though I am told that it is quite delicious."

The coffee and liquor arrived with some unusual mint sticks that complimented the whole meal in a manner that could only be described as miraculous.

Feeling by now rather sleepy, Sarah said good night and went back to her room. Glancing at the clock, she was surprised to see that it was now after 10-30 pm. Where had the evening gone?

By now, nothing about this most incredible place would surprise her, or so she thought. But finding the bed turned down and her most comfortable night wear laid out was beyond belief for such an out of the way unknown hotel. After cleaning her teeth and removing her makeup, though she wore very little, she slid into bed, again finding that everything was as right as it could be. Her last thoughts as she pulled the covers over her was that this is the place she had dreamed of so many years ago when suffering at the hands of her thoughtless parents and even more thoughtless neighbours.

CHAPTER FOUR

She woke the next morning after a night filled with dreams that she knew had been rather exotic but just could not remember any details. Odd about that she thought, you wake up sure you would remember good dreams but usually by the time you have been awake for a few minutes all the memories are gone. It's only the bad dreams that stay with you. I daresay some clever 'trick cyclist' could explain it all away. Nevertheless, she felt bright and alive to a degree beyond her expectations. She also felt hungry.

She showered, brushed her hair and dressed in a comfortable plain white blouse and dark grey slacks. Finding she had a need to go for a walk after her breakfast, she slipped on a comfortable pair of walking shoes which she could not remember packing and went down to the dining room. She had decided not to wear any makeup and was just going through the door when Keith appeared with a napkin over his arm, also dressed as if to go walking.

He asked if she would like breakfast.

Surprising herself with her appetite, Sarah said,

"I usually have just cereal and coffee but somehow I fancy some eggs and bacon, with fresh tomatoes, well cooked, so the skin falls off, brown bread and butter and more of that beautiful coffee."

"Your wish is my command."

Keith smiled that so innocent and infectious smile and off he went into the kitchen.

The breakfast food when it arrived was as good as it looked and better than she could have imagined. Again, as with dinner the previous evening, she felt full but not stuffed and after a short while decided a walk would be in order.

Leaving the side door, Sarah walked towards the road way circumnavigating the green and without any hesitation she turned right towards the church. As she did so, a rather rotund policeman on a bicycle that would not have looked out of place in a museum, trundled past.

"Morning Miss. Trust you have settled in all right, very comfortable hotel that is. The best around these parts."

Now how the hell did he know I was staying at the hotel and she could not imagine there were many others in the immediate area, if any at all.

Wondering about this she was nonetheless polite enough to reply,

"It certainly is a comfortable place officer, good of you to ask."

"That's O.K Miss. I like to know who and where people are hereabouts. They call me Sid by the way, been serving this village and three more like it for the past twenty years, as did my dad and his dad before that. A bit of an institution I suppose you might say but it helps knowing everyone who lives here and who are the visitors. Good day to you, enjoy your walk."

With that, he was on his cycle and heading towards the pub near the church.

'Good grief,' she thought. What a strange set up. The same policeman, from the same family, over three generations.

Continuing her walk towards the church with the intention of going inside, she noticed a small lane to the left of the wall. It was tidy and had a neat sign which read,

Memory lane, foot path only.

CHAPTER FIVE

Sarah found herself almost hurrying to turn into this slight detour to her plans. Still, into the lane she went finding that for the first few hundred yards it was brick paved and aligned with a multitude of small flowers. These differed in colour like beds of the 'Hundreds and Thousands' sweets that she would buy as a child with the money she stole from her mother's purse.

Then suddenly the path opened onto a wider section that was virtually a roadway but obviously never had traffic on it. It was truly beautiful.

But the strangest thing of all was that walking towards her was Keith.

"Hello," he said. "Fancy meeting you here, a lovely surprise though. I was just on my way and saw you emerge from the narrow part of the walk. Lovely here, I often stroll here in the mornings. It's such a peaceful place. It's so easy to unwind and forget all your troubles. May I walk with you?"

Before Sarah had chance to collect her thoughts she said,

"Of course you can, I would be delighted with the company."

With that they began their journey together, not knowing or perhaps understanding why but Sarah was certain it was the right thing to do. She felt so comfortable with Keith, as if she had known him all her life. She began to see more flowers of so many varieties all in full bloom. Her mind began to wander back in time to her life during those first few years after the rape.

The trauma for a while wondering if she might be pregnant, the relief when her time came round again and she knew she was not but raging against the tide of a life that had allowed such a terrible thing to happen to her. She knew that somehow she would get her revenge on as many men as she could.

Her first forays into the world of connivance and she supposed blackmail. As each stupid man came along, for that was how she began to think of them, she would inveigle them into situations that compromised them and then would demand money, clothes, and jewellery. Never overdoing the value and after a while she could judge just how much her marks were worth. She never asked for more than they could give, always keeping to her word that it would be a one off donation to her well-being. It did not stop her victims from worrying but after a period of time they all realised that she would not ask for more than her original demands.

It had worked well and as her standard of life improved so did her contacts. She discovered one day that a man she was with was really asking to be punished for his wrongdoing. She had obliged him with smacking him with her hair brush. He was so turned on sexually but had no desire to further the experience by wanting sex with her. He had thanked her profusely and given her a rather handsome fee.

This had started her on the road to arranging bondage nights with those strange men who just wanted to be treated to pain. Some of them required the dressing up by her into costumes ranging from nurses to school girls. It provided an income that was far beyond the petty donations from minor embarrassed husbands. The big bonus was that she did not have to sleep with any of them. Though her intense hate of men in general had diminished considerably, there was still that underlying element that despised all men. A few men friends had come along the way but Sarah had never enjoyed the physical side of her relationships and they usually went on their way after a few weeks disillusioned and with the thought that perhaps she was a lesbian after all.

She had no passion.

These thoughts were trickling through her mind when she became aware that here she was, with a rather good looking man, walking down a strange road in a strange village and she was enjoying the moment immensely. Keith was close but she was feeling that she wanted him closer, wanted him to take her hand and put his arm around her. Her whole being was crying out for attention from him.

Her thoughts were suddenly awake and she realised that he was walking along with his arm around her waist.

'When did that happen? But God it was a lovely feeling, please don't take your arm away.' she said to herself.

Leaning into him, they slowly strolled along like a pair of long time lovers. She felt so in time with him it was as if time itself was of no concern. She just did not want the moment to end.

'Why now? I really thought this could not happen to me. Why am I so happy just to be here with man who I only met yesterday? Yet I am.'

"May I call you Sarah?"

"Do. Oh please do."

"I was just wondering Sarah, if you had noticed the type of flowers that are lining the road at this point."

She looked up and across to the sides of the road and all she could see for miles ahead was sunflowers. There were hundreds of them but as she looked she fancied she could determine certain lines that had the semblance of faces in them. Several of the centres of the sunflowers were faces of past men she had swindled, coerced, conned, or simply stolen from. It was unnerving and she broke away from Keith's arm, she was staring and almost in tears.

She was in tears.

"Whatever is the problem?" Keith asked. "You look very upset about something. You can tell me you know, I won't judge."

Sarah was beginning to pull herself together and realise it was all an illusion but it had thrown her for a short while and she felt she wanted some comfort from Keith.

He put his arms about her and held her close. Sarah relaxed more completely than she had ever before. It was as if her entire life had been just a prelude to this moment. Her whole body wanted nothing more than to be loved by this man and her mind was going round in circles imagining all the loving moves that had never happened to her to now begin.

Her eyes opened and she was lying on the grass in an isolated part of the countryside. Alongside her was Keith, this oh so wonderful man whom she had waited all her previous existence for. She pulled him to her and she could feel his whole body against hers. His chest, the front of his muscular thighs, his head was by her head, she was dizzy with the need for him.

They were undressed and they were making love. Not since the rape had she had a man inside her. This was so different, this was sublime ecstasy and this was everything she had avoided for so long. But this was Keith. This was the man she could, would not do without.

How long they lay there she could not say. There was no desire to look at her watch, wanting to stay locked together for always.

"We should get back for dinner at least," Keith muttered in her ear.

"What did you say? I don't want to move."

"Maybe, but that is about all we have been doing for the past few hours and I don't really want to move either but it could start to get dark soon and we have a fairly long walk back."

With reluctance they parted and rearranged their clothing and walked back to the hotel arm in arm as true lovers do. Sarah was in a dream world she could not fully understand but wanted so much more of it from this incredible man.

Parting at the door to the hotel they went to their respective rooms, showered and changed. They went down to dinner, he to serve and her to be served Again she was ravenous, Keith was naturally much more attentive than before. She noticed the old couple in the corner eating away and this time they waved and smiled a knowing sort of smile, almost grinning with delight at seeing her.

'They know,' she thought. 'They know what Keith and I have been doing all day. But I am so happy that I do not care, in fact I am glad they know. I want to tell the whole world I am in love.'

And she was in love.

The next few days were spent in Keith's company. He moved into her room and they made love as often as possible. They were insatiable but all things must come to an end and so, after ten days of a happiness she had not dreamed of, the time arrived when she must go. There were things in her life that had to be cleared up before her dreams could be fully realised.

Saying good bye to Keith's father, she left and started on her way back to her flat to finalise her new life.

NOT QUITE THE END

After a while, the road was covered with police and fire officers and paramedics who continued to arrive at the scene of the accident where the overturned lorry and the smashed cars now lay smoking and steaming.

The ill-fated driver of the lorry was placed carefully into the ambulance as were several others including the woman who had been presumed dead by one of the other car drivers. She was seriously injured but alive.

The police took details of and brief statements from everyone who had been involved. The dog was allowed to be taken away by the woman who had thought to rescue it, on the understanding that it would be restored to the owner or her dependants as soon as was practicable.

The whole scene was dealt with in an efficient manner and everyone was told that they would be contacted at a later date for a full statement and may be called as witnesses at court.

During this time, three of the men and one of the women had talked amongst themselves and had all mentioned where they had come from that day, a village called Tumbleford.

It created some concern as they began to relate their individual stories and discover that they had all been there at the same time.

One of the men said,

"Hang on this can't be right. We have all been there at the same time but never saw each other. That's ridiculous. I've got a map in my car so we can compare notes."

Off he went and came back a few moments later with a rather out of date and old Esso road map. Laying it out on the bonnet of one of the other cars, he attempted to find this illusive place called Tumbleford. But try as he might, it was not to be found.

"Bloody strange. I know it was there because this map is the one I used to find the village in the first place. It's the only map I have in the car."

By this time all four of them were beginning to have doubts as to whether they had actually been there at all. The woman, who felt less agitated than the men, leant back against one of the remaining cars. All felt they had been tricked somehow but could not understand how or even why this would be so. They had never met before and so had no reason to believe that any prank could link them together in such a complicated manner.

Yet their individual descriptions of the village tied in so well that they all felt convinced it had been true. They had all been there at the same time and at the same place. They had seemingly stayed in the same hotel, but never met.

This was not possible.

At last one of the men said,

"Well, it's all a big mystery and if you will excuse me I am off before I become convinced that I am going bonkers or have been on some illusionary drug trip. I am going home and will try to forget that we ever met. As for the time spent there at Tumbleford, whether it was real or not, I can only say that it was great and I definitely spent the last few days somewhere. Good bye to you all, maybe we will never meet again. Enjoy the rest of your lives."

With that, off he strode to his car. He got in and drove away south towards London. The other two men did the same but in different directions.

The woman lingered for a time till they had gone. Then she slowly walked to her own car and climbed in. She gave a really broad and very happy smile, a sigh of absolute contentment. Then she turned sideways and gave the man in the passenger seat a very affectionate kiss.

She said, "I feel so much happier than they seem to be. I love you so much Keith. Let's begin our lives together."

www.ingramcontent.com/pod-product-compliance
Lightning Source LLC
Chambersburg PA
CBHW022155170626
46807CB00005B/2221